Caught By the Dragon

Maiden to the Dragon, Book 1

Mac Flynn

All names, places, and events depicted in this book are fictional and products of the author's imagination.

No part of this publication may be reproduced, stored in a retrieval system, converted to another format, or transmitted in any form without explicit, written permission from the publisher of this work. For information regarding redistribution or to contact the author, write to the publisher at the following address.

Crescent Moon Studios, Inc.
P.O. Box 117
Riverside, WA 98849

Website: www.macflynn.com
Email: mac@macflynn.com

ISBN / EAN-13: 9781791892470

Copyright © 2018 by Mac Flynn

First Edition

CONTENTS

Chapter 1..1
Chapter 2..7
Chapter 3..11
Chapter 4..19
Chapter 5..27
Chapter 6..34
Chapter 7..40
Chapter 9..53
Chapter 10..60
Chapter 11..68
Chapter 12..77
Chapter 13..86
Chapter 14..93
Chapter 15..98

Continue the adventure...................................105
Other series by Mac Flynn............................113

CAUGHT BY THE DRAGON

CHAPTER 1

"Weekend at last!"

That was my cry as I stretched my arms above my head. Around me were throngs of my coworkers. We left the fifty-floor office building in a giant herd of tired and eager humanity.

"Amen!" one of them called out.

"Anybody seeing the game?" another one asked.

"I'm just seeing my eyelids," a hefty guy quipped.

That got a laugh from we office-dwellers, a laugh that extinguished much of the exhaustion from a lot of faces. I stepped out onto the wide, busy sidewalk and glanced around me. The front doors spilled out onto a major intersection, and all around me bustled a humanity eager to get home to family and dinner. I only had the dinner part, but pizza awaited me.

Still, being among such a large crowd of my fellow humans was a bitter reminder of how normal my boring life was.

"Hey, Mir!" I glanced to my left. My friend from the office, Heather, waved to me. Beside her was a cute guy I'd seen in our office, a recent transfer from some other large company. My heart sank. "Over here, Mir!" I slapped a smile on my face and walked over to them. Heather turned to the guy and jerked her head toward me. "This is the sexy woman I've been telling you about, Blake."

Blake looked me over. There was something dark about his eyes that I didn't like. He held out his hand. "Nice to meet you."

I shook the hand. His fingers were clammy like his skin didn't quite fit. "Likewise, and don't let Heather tell you about my bed life. It's practically non-existent."

Heather rolled her eyes. "Come on, do you both have to be so old-fashioned with the handshake? I'm trying to hook you up here."

Blake laughed. "I don't think this is going to work, Heth. She's on to me."

Heather blinked at him. "On to you?"

He shook his head. "It's nothing. Anyway, nice to have met you." He waved and walked off.

I turned to my friend. "This is the third time this month, and it's only the seventh day."

She sighed and shrugged. "I'm just trying to get you hooked. You're too nice not to deserve a good man and reproduce."

I glanced at Blake's retreating back and pursed my lips. "Then stop trying to help me. The guys you keep showing me are getting creepier."

CAUGHT BY THE DRAGON

Heather followed my gaze. "I don't think he was that bad. A little strange, yeah, but who isn't?" She turned back to see me ten feet away and gaining ground. "Hey! Wait up!" She hurried after me and came up to my side. "Wanna get a bite to eat before you hole yourself in your apartment for the weekend?"

I grinned. "Only if you're buying."

Heather rolled her eyes. "Fine, fine, but I expect to get a dance out of this."

I cringed as we walked side-by-side down the sidewalk. "You know I hate that."

"The only way you'll dance is with someone you know, and I'll probably be the only one you know," she pointed out.

"Then how about we skip the dancing?"

"Nope. I need the exercise." Heather stepped onto the street and raised her hand. "Taxi!" She glanced back at me. "Besides, it's good practice for when you get married. The bride's gotta dance at her wedding, you know."

I sighed as a taxi drove up. "You're impossible."

We slipped into the taxi. Heather leaned forward. "To the Bar Room, and step on it. We need to get drunk."

The driver smiled and nodded. "Yes, ma'am." He pulled us off the curb and into traffic.

Heather fell back against the seat and looked to me. "Speaking of losing weight, I was thinking of going hiking one of these weekends with a few other girls. Wanna come with?"

I shook my head. "I'm not much for nature walks."

She frowned. "It's the society, isn't it?"

I winced. "It's not that. It's just-well, I just don't feel like I fit in. Like I'm an outsider or something, you know what I mean?"

Heather shook her head. "No, and I won't take 'no' for an answer the next time I ask you to go with me on an adventure. You need to live a little, Miriam, before your whole life is gone."

I glanced out the window and sighed. The world sped by us as a shadow play of colorful lights and figures. "I know. I. . .I just feel like I'm supposed to wait for something. Like my time will come."

The taxi driver's loud voice interrupted us. "Hey, ladies. I think someone's following you."

"Really?" Heather wondered as we both turned and looked through the rear window.

The taxi driver nodded. "Yeah, that red one.

Heather glanced at our driver. "You sure it's not for you?"

He shrugged. "I don't know. I ain't picked up no one but you in the last half hour."

Heather squealed and clapped her hands. "You think you can lose 'em?"

The driver grinned. "No problem, but for the risk it'll be extra."

"I'll take that risk!" my friend accepted.

I whipped my head to her. "Wait a-ah!" The driver turned a sharp corner onto a side street. I was sent into the waiting arms of my laughing friend.

"Isn't this great?" she yelled.

"Yeah, wonderful," I replied as I extracted myself from her arms. "It's going to be great sitting in jail, too."

"This is living!" Heather gleefully exclaimed.

The driver took another sharp corner into an alley and sped up. I clutched the oh-shit handle above my door. "This isn't living! This is the preliminaries before death!"

"Just enjoy the ride already!" she insisted.

We took another ninety-degree corner that sent my stomach reeling. "I want out!"

"Just another block, misses!" the driver shouted as he weaved through traffic and onto another bumpy alley.

"Let me out now!" I yelled.

Heather pointed at the alley intersection ahead of us. "Stop there and we'll get out. Then book it like we're still aboard."

"What about my fare?" he reminded us.

She grabbed some cash from her pocket and tossed the bills into the seat beside him. "That should cover it."

His eyes flickered to the catch and he grinned. "Yes, ma'am!"

He slammed on the brake. I slid forward an inch before my seat belt dug into my skin. The car slid to a stop in the center of the intersection.

Heather tore off her seat belt, unbuckled mine, threw open the door and pulled me out. "Thanks for the fun!"

The driver saluted us and sped off a second after Heather slammed the door shut. She tugged me into the side alley and behind a large dumpster. We crouched down as a car sped down the perpendicular alley. The black car zoomed past us and continued to follow our former taxi.

Heather jumped to her feet and wiped her arm across her brow. "Wow, that was close."

I stood on my shakier legs and grasped the edge of the dumpster. My stomach was in tumbling knots. I staggered past her and down the alley that we'd come.

Heather reached out for me. "Hey, wait! Where are you going?"

I didn't look back. "Home."

"But what about finding a guy at the bar?" she reminded me.

"I need to find my stomach back here first," I quipped. "Then maybe I'll call you tomorrow about bar-hopping."

Heather stamped her foot on the ground and slopped puddle water all over herself. "Fine! If you don't want my help then go and find your own guy!"

I waved to her without looking back. It wasn't such a bad suggestion if Fate hadn't had other plans.

CAUGHT BY THE DRAGON

CHAPTER 2

The bus commute took longer than I hoped, so I didn't get to my apartment building until forty-five minutes after the harrowing taxi incident. Night beat me to the stoop of my apartment building, and with it came its friends shadow and darkness. The bus stop was half a block away from where I lived, so I had to walk past rows of apartment buildings to get to mine. An alley separated my building from a neighboring one.

The streets were deserted as I made my way down the sidewalk. I reached the alley and paused. Had I heard something clattering around in there? I leaned forward and squinted into the darkness. Hulking shadows of trashcans and broken boxes stared back at me. Puddles reflected the darkness that was only broken by a few feeble attempts by the streetlights to illuminate the deep interior.

Nothing moved. Nothing clattered. I shrugged and kept going to the stoop. My keys rattled in my hand as I drew them from my purse.

I froze. A rattle had mimicked my own. I half-turned and looked at the mouth of the dark alley. Something flickered in the corner of my sight, but disappeared before I could catch a full, telling glimpse.

My pulse quickened. I fumbled with my key chain. The damn key wouldn't come out. There! It separated from the others. I shoved it into the lock. A quick turn and I fell inside. I slammed the door behind me. The entrance rattled and the noise echoed through the lonely lobby.

I grasped my chest and tried to catch my breath. "Easy there, Miriam. It was just your imagination. . ." I whispered to myself.

Still, I couldn't shake the feeling of being watched. I hurried up the stairs to my private abode.

My one-bedroom apartment was on the third floor with a lovely view of the fire escape and the neighboring brick building. I tossed my purse onto the small table beside the door and plopped into my favorite-and only-recliner. The sensation of being watched faded within the confines of my locked apartment.

My aching feet thanked me as I leaned back and closed my eyes. "Now this is the way to live. . ." I murmured. "Just me and my chair."

I noticed a sweet smell in the apartment which was unusual. None of my incense candles were lit. I tried to rise from my chair, but my arms wouldn't pull me forward.

The feeling of being watched returned. Movement caught my eye. I glanced at the window to the fire escape.

CAUGHT BY THE DRAGON

Three figures stood on the other side of the glass. I gasped, but the scream stuck in my throat.

One of the figures knelt in front of the window and fidgeted with the bottom of the sill. The window popped up an inch. The person drew it to the top and slipped inside. The other two followed.

The overhead light allowed me to see the intruders. Two were burly men in ragged overcoats, pants, and shirts. They were followed by a familiar face. Blake.

The ragged pair strode over to me. One grabbed my legs and the other pulled a rope from his coat. Together they began to bind my legs.

I couldn't fight. I couldn't even let out more than a garbled whisper. Blake moved to stand by my head. My terrified eyes looked up into his smiling face.

He leaned down and studied my face. "What a lucky break your friend introduced me to you today. You're just in time to join a few other girls on an exciting journey."

One of the burly men snorted. "Yeah. A regular cruise line."

"With all expenses paid," the other one joined in.

Blake straightened and chuckled. "Come, come, my dear fellows. It's an honor for this young woman to join in this age-old ritual." His eyes flickered back to me and the smile slipped a little. "She may even be good enough to be *his* consort."

"She ain't pretty enough," one of his cohorts commented.

Blake closed his eyes and shook his head. "Beauty isn't everything, my friend, and I think this one might have something special about her. After all-" he leaned down close to me again and reached into his shirt collar. My eyes widened as he pulled away the fake flesh that clung tightly to his brown skin. The nostrils of his nose bulged out like that of a pig, and his teeth were yellow and sharp at the ends like fangs. He was a monster. "-she saw through my disguise."

I wanted to run. I wanted to push him away. All I could manage was a shudder.

"Stop fooling around and help us," one of the men insisted.

Blake tucked the mask back into his collar and grinned. "All right, but don't damage the merchandise."

"What about knocking her out? She's going to struggle," another pointed out.

Blake pulled a cloth from his pocket. A stench similar to rotten plants attacked my nostrils. "I'll take care of that now. It'll prove whether she's one of them or not, too."

He shoved the cloth over my mouth and nose. The horrible smell invaded my senses. My body still wouldn't respond. Its only reaction were tears that pooled in my eyes and slid down my cheeks. My furious thoughts gave way to a loose grasp of consciousness. My head began to spin along with the room.

In a moment I was knocked clean out.

CHAPTER 3

"Let me out! God damn fucks! Let me out!"

My dark world was slowly receding, and that was my introduction back into the real one. I forced my eyes open and was presented with a barren sight.

I was in the back of a metal truck. The floor and walls were plates of steel, but the ceiling was made of canvas. The rear of the truck was also canvas and tied so tightly not a single bit of light could be seen behind us. I heard the tires crunch on gravel and the up-and-down motion of the truck told me we were driving over short hills.

On either side were long wooden benches, and it was on one of these that I sat, but I wasn't alone. Beside and opposite me were four other women, all roughly around my age. They all had their hands bound behind their back and their ankles were captured in chains. I shifted and chains rattled on my own feet.

The one who pounded against the side of the truck was a woman with a scowling face. Tears had ran her makeup down her face and given her an undead look. She slammed her shoulder into the wall and winced, but her furious expression didn't abate.

"Let me out, you stupid fucks!" she screamed.

"Will you stop that?" one of the women to my left snapped. "You've been trying that for fifteen minutes and whoever's driving the truck hasn't even slowed down. They don't give a damn."

Mascara-face sneered at her. "You idiots can just sit there, but I'm not going to give up. Maybe somebody else will hear me.' She took a deep breath and opened her big mouth wide. "Heellppppp!"

The truck slowed down. Mascara-face sat up and grinned. "See? I get results."

Everyone quieted as the truck stopped. A door opened and heavy boots hit the gravel. They walked along the side of the truck to the rear where the canvas was untied. The cloth was shoved aside and revealed Blake in all his piggy glory. Behind him stretched a vast forest of thick trees. The shroud of night hung over the forest. The gravel road wound through it, and up and over the short hills. Distant lights spoke of a small town, but nothing like the city I knew.

He sneered at all of us. "What the hell's going on here?"

Mascara-face gathered what few wits she had and glared at him. "I-I want you to release me."

CAUGHT BY THE DRAGON

Blake snorted. The noise even sounded piggish. "Like hell we will. You just shut up, will you? We can't hear ourselves think up there."

"What do you want with us?" the woman beside me questioned him.

Blake chuckled. "You'll see. We should be there in a little bit, and then you'd better keep your mouths shut. The lords don't like loud women unless they're bedding them."

He dropped the canvas and tied it back. A terrible hush fell over us as he marched back to the front. The truck started forward down the gravel road.

A few sniffles broke the silence.

"Will you guys shut up already?" the irate woman snapped. She glanced in my direction. "What are you looking at?"

I frowned and looked to my right. A girl of maybe twenty sat beside me. Her shoulders shook and soft sobs escaped her lips.

I leaned my shoulder against her. She looked up at me. "You okay?"

The girl shook her head. She wiped her face and swallowed. "W-where are they taking us? Why did they take us?"

I pursed my lips and shook my head. "I don't know. What do you last remember?"

"We've all got the same story," the irate one spoke up. She swept her eyes over our little group and sneered at them. "Everybody was grabbed out of their homes or off the streets by those creeps and drugged. We all woke up in this truck, nobody knows what's going on, and that little brat's been crying since she woke up."

I glared at her. "You don't have to be an asshole. We're all going through this together, so we should stick together."

"You're dreaming," she snapped back as she nodded her head in the direction we'd traveled. "Did you see all those trees? I'm not going to be dragging a brat with me. She'll only slow me down."

"It's the only way we're going to be able to get away from those pig boys," I shot back.

She sneered at me. "It's everybody for themselves. Besides, I didn't see anybody helping me make noise."

"That's enough, you two. We're not getting anywhere with this arguing," the fifth woman spoke up.

"Yeah, I guess I am wasting my time here," the irate woman retorted.

The second woman glared at her, but turned to me. "Some of us introduced ourselves before you two woke up. Mind telling us your names?"

"Miriam," I told her.

"My name's Alexandra, but you can call me Alex," she introduced herself. She nodded at my younger charge and the other quieter woman. "That's Stephanie and Cindy."

"What's the point of telling each other about ourselves?" the other one spoke up.

Alex rolled her eyes and jerked her head towards our less-amiable companion. "That's Olivia."

"You're just wasting your time getting to know each other. For all we know they're going to sell us to sex slavers and we're never going to see anybody again," Olivia scolded her.

"It'll help if some of us get out of here and tell police who we met," Alex argued.

CAUGHT BY THE DRAGON

Someone pounded a fist against the back of the cab. "Shut up back there!" Blake called through the thin plate.

I shifted in my chains. They wouldn't budge. There was a thin hole in one of my feet bracelets. "Anybody know how to pick a lock?"

"If one of us did we'd be out of here," Olivia pointed out.

We grew quiet again. There was only the sound of the wheels as they ground against the gravel. The truck swayed more heavily from side-to-side, and in a few minutes we slowed to a stop.

The engine shut off, and two doors were opened and slammed shut. Three sets of feet walked along the sides of the truck, and the rear flap was thrown aside. Blake revealed himself and his two compatriots. Their human faces, too, were gone and their snout-nosed true identities were revealed.

Blake stepped aside and jerked his head toward the road. "Climb out of there." We hesitated and glanced at each other. "Climb out, or we drag you out."

Cindy stood, and we others followed. One-by-one we shuffled out in single file. Stephanie was ahead of me. She hesitated at the edge of the bed. It was two feet to the ground, and our shackles didn't help with climbing.

One of the men grabbed her arm and yanked her down. "Come on! We don't have all day!"

Stephanie cried out and fell onto her side onto the ground. A flash of red blinded my vision. I screamed and lunged at the closest asshole. My shoulder connected with his face and we both toppled to the gravel.

Alex gave a war whoop and threw herself at the other henchman. Cindy charged Blake. He side-stepped her attack and smacked her on the back of her head. Cindy's eyes rolled back in her head and she crumpled to the ground.

"Handle these wenches or you're fired!" he snapped at the other two pig-men.

My victim wrapped me in a tight bear hug and stood. Alex, likewise, was subdued. Blake stalked over to us and glared first at Alex and then me.

His eyes narrowed at me. "You two are almost more trouble than you're worth. One more stupid move like that and you'll be thrown out into this world that you wouldn't last five minutes in." He turned to his henchmen and the other cowering girls, and swept his arm toward to his right. "Get them inside before they're all sick and wasted."

My eyes followed his arm. Before us not more than twenty feet stood a long, stone-built stable. The thatched gable roof and foggy, primitive windows bespoke a rustic lifestyle.

Beyond the stable stretched a hundred acres of open ground surrounded by the forest. The ground was level except the extreme right side where it sloped off into the forest and a glen.

A large castle occupied five front acres of the ground. Its tall battlements cast their long shadows over the smaller stable and our crowd. Six towers at the four corners and center of the long battlements accented the rectangular design of the stone structure. Soft lights lit up the tall, narrow windows that looked out on green fields and pastures. Cows and sheep grazed in their own fences, and a large fenced area was connected to the wall of the stables opposite where we stood.

The gravel road passed by the castle and dipped down a little on its journey back into the woods, but a part of it branched off to the front of the castle. The road traveled through an imposing stone arch with two massive doors. They were hewn from mighty trees, and on their surface were carved figures I couldn't quite make out.

I glanced over my shoulder. Behind us was a small village of stone huts with thatched roofs. The homes were nestled on both sides of the road, and from their stone chimneys poured forth smoke. Flickering lights behind the foggy window glass reflected long shadows of the occupants. A few of them were those who traveled in and out of the high castle.

"Get on with ya!" one of the henchman snapped.

I was shoved forward and made to fall in line with the other girls. Each of the men snatched an oil lantern from the cab of the truck and lit our path. We were marched into the large door of the stables and to three empty stalls at the end closest to the gate. Alex, Stephanie, and I were shoved into one stall and the other three were tossed into the other.

Blake stood between the stalls and sneered at us. "Take the manacles off all the girls except those two troublemakers, and then go check to see if they're ready up there."

One of his companions frowned. "But that'll make 'em look lame for the presentation."

Blake grinned. "Some of our buyers like them bound."

The three of them laughed at the crude joke as they unlocked the manacles, but the hands remained tied behind their backs. Alex and I were passed over, but I was glad when Stephanie's ankles were freed. One of the pig-men disappeared through a door at the end of the stables.

Blake glanced from one stall to the other. "Now listen up. I won't be repeating this. You lot are to be presented to some very influential-" he chuckled, "-we'll call them men.

Some of them will want to take you. You'd better hope they do, otherwise you're discarded to the servant's quarters of this castle and left there to fend for yourself." He paced the floor between the straw of the stalls. "If you're good girls you'll be chosen and given a life of luxury in their homes."

"But I want to go home!" Stephanie insisted.

He stopped his pacing and sneered at her. "Nobody gets back through the Portal. Nobody." His sly grin slipped onto his lips. "At least not alive."

"What the hell are you talking about? What portal?" Alex questioned him.

"That's for you girls to find out, but after you're presented to the Lords of the Air," he replied.

"But we just want to go home!" one of the women yelled.

"Please take us home!" Stephanie pleaded.

"Let us go!" Alex demanded.

"Shut up!" Blake snapped. His pork snout flared in and out as he glared at each of us. "You're staying here, so stop you're whining and get used to it!"

The door opened a sliver and the henchman slipped inside. He moved to stand beside Blake and glanced over his shoulder before he spoke in a whispered voice. "We've got a problem."

Blake narrowed his eyes. "What kind of problem?"

A soft female voice spoke up. "There is no problem."

CAUGHT BY THE DRAGON

CHAPTER 4

The door opened wider and a hooded figure stepped inside. Her silk cloak shimmered in the dim light of the three lanterns. In her hand she held a more elegant, silver-edged lamp. She threw off her hood and revealed herself as a woman of seventy. Her long silver hair trailed down her back in a long braid, and her wrinkles perfectly suited her firm demeanor. She stood between the stalls and held her lamp up to look at us.

The woman frowned and her eyes flickered to Blake. "You have been warned before not to treat the girls poorly."

Blake smiled and shrugged. "This was out of our control. Some of the women tried to escape."

She nodded at the manacles on my feet. "Remove those."

He frowned and shook his head. "I refuse. If these girls escape it'll be my wallet that's on the line, not yours. If you have a problem with it then take it up with your master, but I'll hear no more of it."

The old woman pursed her lips, but turned her attention to us. "You must all be very frightened and confused. I tell you there is no need. You have been chosen to be trained as Maidens to the dragon lords, the rulers of this realm. They will chose one of you to be their confidante."

Olivia snorted. "You're joking, right?"

The old woman's steady gaze fell on her. She shrank beneath those old eyes, and the woman continued. "One of you will have the honor of being Maiden to the Grand Dragon Lord himself. If the dragon lord who chooses you finds you a worthy mate you will be made his wife and never want for anything till the end of your days."

"But I just want to go home," Stephanie insisted.

Blake took a step toward her and curled his lips back. "I told you you can't go back, now-" The woman raised her hand. He snapped his mouth shut and sullenly retreated to the background.

The woman knelt in front of Stephanie. "Once you have crossed into these realms and been Marked you can never go back. That is not a rule, but a law of nature. To go back to your world means death to you."

Stephanie burst into tears. Alex wiggled up beside her and smiled. "It'll be okay."

The woman stood and looked over us. "You shall be chosen this night. May the gods grant you the future you wish." She bowed to us and strode from the stables.

CAUGHT BY THE DRAGON

Blake stepped forward and swept his arm over us. "Get them up!"

We were yanked to our feet and positioned in two columns shoulder-to-shoulder with one of our fellow captives. I had Stephanie beside me. She hung her head and sniffled.

I nudged her shoulder with mine and smiled when she looked up at me. "It'll be all right. We'll think of-"

"March!" Blake barked.

They led us out the wide door at the end and into a small courtyard that separated the stables from a side door in the castle. The front gate stood to our far right, and people and carriages loitered within the walls in a larger courtyard. The people wore simple leather and cloth clothes like they were from the Middle Ages. Men in armor with lances in their hands guarded either side of the gate. Their helmets were tipped with leather-looking wings. On some of their chest plates was a side view of a green wing superimposed over a blue circle. Others had single bands of colors of gold, brown, black, and white.

One of the henchmen shoved me forward. "Stop gawking and get moving."

We were marched through the tight door and into a narrow passage. The floor and walls were made of stone smoothed over the ages by foot traffic and shoulder brushing. Our shoulders bumped into each other as Blake led the way down the hall and past several open doorways. I caught a glimpse of more hallways and a large kitchen with a billowing wood stove. A dozen women in white aprons scurried to and fro baking and stirring. Their chatter soothed my ears. It was a glimpse of the familiar in an unfamiliar place.

We reached the end of the hall. A winding staircase of stone led around a column to the higher levels of the castle. We marched up the long steps. My chains rattled against the hard stone. I stumbled and knocked my shoulder into the wall to my right.

The henchman behind me grabbed my bruised shoulder and shoved me back onto my feet. "Get on now! Get on!"

The long walk led us past one archway and to the third floor of the huge castle. We stepped off onto a wide passage. Burning torches hung from their cages along the walls and lit the dark spaces. Wide, thick wood doors stood on either side of the hall. A sound of laughing and stringed instruments echoed down the hall from a pair of open doors.

It was to them that Blake led us. He entered a feasting hall to loud cheers and applause. The sound came from dozens of men who sat on wood benches arranged in three long rows. Women adorned in white aprons served them with drink and food. They wore rough cloaks and furs, and many sported beards.

The noise became deafening when we were marched in behind him. Many of them stood and raised their large mugs to us.

Others raised a toast to the five men at the front of the room to our left. They were seated behind a long table set up on a wooden podium above the stone floor. Their chairs had high backs upon which were draped five different colors of clothes. They ranged in age from twenty to sixty, and their silk clothes were the same color as the cloths on their chairs. The oldest sported white hair, and another one wore his hair long and over his shoulders. A thin man of forty with a dark complexion leered at us.

CAUGHT BY THE DRAGON

The man who sat in the center of the was about thirty with short, spiked dirty-blond hair and green eyes. He sat at attention with one hand over his lips. His eyes studied each of us with a firm, steady gaze that didn't betray his emotions. Behind him was draped a cloth of blue and green. It was the only one with more than one color.

We were arranged single-file before the five men and faced them. Blake scurried over to the table and bowed low before the men. "My Lords, I present to you my most recent offering, and the likes of which have not been seen in a thousand years."

"That's for us to decide," one of the men, the long-haired burly man with a brown beard, countered. His cloth color was a dull brown.

Blake smiled and nodded. "Indeed, My Lords, and decide you shall." He stepped to the side and swept his arm over our little group. "All of them are strong, healthy females willing and able to please you in all the ways of the world." A great laugh arose from the heathens behind us.

One of the men leaned over the table and studied us. "They look a little skinny this year. Is that world not feeding their women?"

Blake bowed to him. "I chose those who would most please you, My Lord."

"Are they truly Maidens?" one of the men, a young lad of maybe twenty-one, wondered.

His wide eyes bespoke his youth as true as his wrinkle-free face and golden, curly locks. Behind him hung a golden cloth. His attention was almost solely on Stephanie, who, though the youngest of us, was one of the prettiest.

Blake chuckled. "I stake my reputation on knowing them by their smell, My Lord. They are each capable of becoming a-"

"Why are two of them still bound?" The speaker was the man in the center. He nodded at Alex and me. "Why have they not been freed of their chains?"

Blake turned to where the lord nodded and sneered at us. "The restraints were necessary, My Lord. They are an unruly pair, perhaps too high-spirited to make much use of besides as horse tamers." The men behind us guffawed.

The brown-bearded one glanced at the center lord. "Well, Grand Dragon Lord, will you not begin this so we may have our fun with them?"

The man addressed as dragon lord dropped his hand and sat at attention. A thin man of fifty scurried from the sidelines of the podium to stand before the men. He wore a blue gown-like suit with green hems. His attire brushed the floor and his long, bell-like sleeves constantly banged against his thin body.

He bowed his head to the leader of the five. "Allow me to assist you, My Lord, in choosing your Maiden."

The dragon lord nodded. "As you wish, Renner."

The old man turned to us and furrowed his brow. He walked the whole line scrutinizing us with his eyes and wrinkled hands. The man lifted our arms and pulled on our hair.

"Ouch!" I yelped when he touched my bruised shoulder.

He frowned at me. "This one appears rather weak, My Lord."

"Get me out of these chains and I'll show you weak," I snapped. The men behind me laughed uproariously.

CAUGHT BY THE DRAGON

Renner's bushy eyebrows crashed down and he shook his head. "A very bad choice. Much too high-spirited." He moved on to Stephanie who stood to my right. A smile slipped onto his dry lips. He spun around and stepped to the side so he could gesture to her before his lord. "I believe this one will be a suitable Maiden, My Lord. She is both beautiful, and delicate."

The dragon lord raised an eyebrow. "She also quivers like a leaf in a storm."

"Ah, but the beauty of this one cannot be compared!" Renner grasped Stephanie's chin and raised her head so she looked at the lord. Her body shook more violently. "And she will grow into self-confidence, My Lord," he added.

My heart pounded. It wasn't hard to judge the youngest of the lords. His soft eyes were captured by her beauty. He only needed his turn to choose her.

The lord pursed his lips, but nodded his head. "Very well. Take her to-"

"Wait!" I spoke up. All eyes turned to me. I stumbled forward. My chains rattled harshly against the stone floor. "Can't you see how scared she is? If you want someone then I'll go in her place!"

The adviser derisively snorted. "What a stupid idea. The Lord has already-"

"A moment, Renner," the dragon lord spoke up. He stood and walked around the table to stand in front of me. I met his red eyes without blinking. "You would take her place? For what design?"

My eyes involuntarily flickered to the youngest of the lords. The dragon lord didn't follow my gaze, but he smiled. "Very well then, I choose you as my Maiden."

"B-but my lord!" the adviser blustered. He scurried forward and waved a hand at me. "She is not the prettiest, and certainly the least controlled!"

The dragon lord half-turned to him. "Then she will suit me." His eyes flickered to Blake. "Unchain my Maiden."

Blake nodded his head like a bobble-doll and stumbled forward. "Of course, My Lord." He fumbled for the keys in his pocket as he knelt in front of me. In a thrice the chains were off.

The Lord turned to his adviser. "Have her taken to her new quarters."

Renner's shriveled shoulders slumped. He sighed and bowed his head. "As you wish, My Lord." He clapped his hands. A pair of guards against the wall hurried forward. He nodded at me. "Take her away."

CAUGHT BY THE DRAGON

CHAPTER 5

The two guards flanked me as they marched me from the room. I glanced over my shoulder and caught a glimpse of Alex and Stephanie before they disappeared behind the wall. My 'escorts' returned me to the stairs and we walked up to the next floor. The hall was a little narrower and the doors smaller and more numerous. They led me to the end of the hall a door short of the last room.

I glanced ahead and to the right, and saw the passage turned right and followed the front of the castle. There were no doors, only the narrow windows that looked out on the road.

One of the guards opened the door, and the other marched me inside. It was a spacious bedroom with a fire place against the far wall. The four-post bed occupied the spare wall to the right of the chimney. Plush sheets and pillows covered the bed. A dresser stood on the wall to my left, and on the opposite wall was a small door.

On the wall to the left of the fireplace, between the bed and hearth, and to the right of the bed were three wide windows with swinging panes. They swung inward as a hole pane, and two of them were open then to allow the sounds of crickets to drift into the room.

A figure stood at the foot of the bed with their back turned to us. When we entered the person turned around, and I recognized the face of the elderly woman from the stables.

Her eyes widened. She glanced at the men and gestured to me. "Is this to be His Lordship's Maiden?"

One of the guards bowed. "Yes, Maid Darda."

She looked back to me and pursed her lips. "Very well. Untie her hands and position yourselves outside the door until Our Lord comes."

The guards bowed and left, shutting the heavy door behind them. The woman circled me and studied me.

"Take a picture. It'll last longer," I quipped.

She stopped in front of me and a smile curled onto her lips. "There are no cameras here, nor the electricity to use such devices."

I frowned. "So is this place in the past?"

"It is, but not in the way you believe." She gestured to the room. "The time in this realm is in sync with that of your world, but the technology hasn't advanced near as far."

I arched an eyebrow. "So what you're trying to tell me is I'm in a different dimension?"

She nodded. "Yes."

I wandered past her to one of the windows. It looked out on the large field and the slope that glided downward to a far-off opening in the trees. "So how'd me and the other girls get here?"

"You would do well to forget that life and think of your new one here," she scolded me.

I turned around and glared at her. "And what's that supposed to mean?"

"You have been chosen for a very honorable position, and even if he does not choose you as a mate you will be given a job for life as a servant in the household," she told me.

"Is that supposed to be a good thing?" I shot back.

She raised an eyebrow. "It very well is, but I see that you are fatigued from your long journey. Perhaps you should lie down for a spell and rest yourself."

"I'm not going to 'lie down for a spell' or do anything that'll make me comfortable," I argued. "This place isn't my home, and never will be."

The corners of her lips twitched upward. "Your thoughts are easy to read. I'm afraid escape is possible from the Castle, but not from the woods. You would not get far without better means of travel than your feet. The communications within the castle are closely guarded, so do not look to the other servants for help. As for outsiders, the nearest human habitation apart from the small village around the castle is over fifteen miles of rough road."

I turned away and grasped the window sill. I didn't want to reveal any sort of escape plan I could devise, if my mind could devise one for me. At the moment it was a little tired, and her suggestion of rest was a little too tempting.

I heard the woman walk across the floor and stop behind me. Her shrunken hand settled on my shoulder. "Forgive me for this."

I frowned and turned toward her. "Forgive you for-ah!" A sharp burning sensation struck my shoulder beneath her palm.

I jerked my shoulder away from her and stumbled back. She lowered her hand to her side and watched me with sorrowful eyes. "The pain will soon subside."

I pulled down my shirt and saw a small, black scorch mark in my flesh. The mark was in the shape of the crest on the guards' armor. I whipped my head up to her. "Are you insane? What did you do to me?"

"Merely the Marking. All Maidens must be marked," she explained.

"You branded me?" I accused her. Even as I spoke the burning sensation simmered to a bruise.

"The Marking is to protect you from other, less scrupulous lords, though the true bonding will take a few hours to complete," she told me. She walked to the door, opened it, and turned to face me. "If you have no other questions, then I will bid you good evening. Tomorrow I will ensure food is brought to you at the appropriate times as you adjust to your new eating schedule."

I glared at her. "How do you expect me to eat when you're branding me all the time?"

She pursed her lips. "The Marking is only done once. As for the meals, the dragon lords are regularly daytime creatures, but during the Marking their schedule will be rather erratic. In time you will learn their peculiarities."

"Not likely. . ." I muttered.

"Pardon?"

"I didn't say anything," I told her.

She bowed her head to me. "Then I will bid you goodnight. Sleep well."

CAUGHT BY THE DRAGON

The woman closed the door and I heard a click of a lock. I turned to face the window and grasped the stone sill once again.

I pulled my sleeve down to hide the mark and rubbed my bruised shoulder. These people were mad. There was no other explanation for their behavior. They believed they were in some fantasy land of lords and ladies with damsels in distress.

I had to get out of here. I had to warn the authorities and help free the others.

I inspected the room for sources of escape. There was the door, but I didn't know where that led. That meant the windows were the best option. I leaned out the open window beside me. The drop was sixty feet to the packed ground. Too far to jump, but not too far to climb down. The numerous sheets on the bed would be my rope.

I went to work pulling and tying. In a half hour I had my rope.

I looked out the window. Nothing stirred but a cool night breeze. There were no sentries pacing the castle grounds. The forest lay a hundred yards off across the expansive fields of animals and one of wheat. I would slip into the trees and double back to follow the road past the village and to civilization, and sanity. These people were obviously mentally ill. Dragon lords and the Maidens? Medieval bullshit. The authorities would come and lock them in an insane asylum.

First, though, the escape. There were other windows below me, and some of the rooms were lit, showing occupation. I slowly lowered my rope out the window and down the castle wall. The rope slid between the two shutters of glass where the borders met, obscuring it from view. The problem would be when my much-wider body slid down.

I secured the rope to the bedstead and paused. Distant sounds were heard, jovial ones. The inmates were celebrating their torment of six women. I had to hurry lest this dragon lord show me off to his drunken friends.

I slipped over the window frame and down the rope. I didn't dare breath. The ground came closer, but so did the other windows. I stopped above one of the illuminated ones. The ground lay twenty feet below me. So close and yet so far. I heard voices from the lit room.

"My Lord, you must see to your guests," I heard Renner's voice insist.

"I have only been away a short while, Renner, and will return in a moment. I'm sure they understand that the danger in the borderlands is more pressing," the dragon lord replied.

"Has something new been heard?" Renner asked him.

"Yes. The scouts have brought news of more raids by these new clans." I heard the faint shuffling of papers followed by the sound of wooden chair legs sliding against rock floor. In a moment a shadow appeared at the window. I held completely still and prayed the rope would do the same. When next he spoke his voice was hardly above a whisper. "Five villages were lost during this last raid."

"And still we know nothing these dragons?" Renner wondered.

"They are barbarians from the north driven down by unknown forces. That is all the scouts could surmise," he told his servant. His shadow moved away from the window.

"Let these matters rest for a while, My Lord, and enjoy yourself. You have been tense far too long," Renner advised.

CAUGHT BY THE DRAGON

A deep sigh came from his master. "Perhaps I have. I will join the others and see their choices. I believe the young Cayden had his eyes set on your favorite."

"Merely an oversight on my part, My Lord. A lapse of bad judgment that shan't happen again," Renner assured him.

In a few moments the candlelight was extinguished and I heard a door shut. Now was my chance. I slid down the remaining distance. My feet touched solid ground and I hunkered down. The grounds remained deserted. They all celebrated their triumph of us and talked their insane talk about rival dragon clans.

CHAPTER 6

I hurried straight across the grounds in a line perpendicular with the castle and rushed into the woods. It was at that moment that I heard shouts from the castle behind me telling me they must have found my empty room and the bedsheets. I rushed down the hill, but chanced a glance over my shoulder. A dozen men poured from the gate with torches in their hands. One of them shouted orders and they spread out across the open grounds and road.

I wanted to see no more, and rushed down the hillside. The path was rocky and muddy from the recent rain, and many times my feet threatened to slip from beneath me. Below me the town twinkled with festive lights, no doubt from the Maiden choosing. The whole place was madness.

The woods weren't as friendly close up as they were from afar. The thick limbs of the ancient trees blocked out the moon, and there were no paths. The brush made my penetrating the forest difficult. Their brambles clawed and scratched at my clothes, tearing and filthying them.

I persevered and thirty feet into the woods I was rewarded with a dirt path made by wild animals. It arced around the perimeter of the castle and followed the road. I followed the path and kept a close eye on the castle, watching for signs of the search team approaching.

The animal path veered from the road, but that was good. A dozen men on horses galloped down the road. By the light of their torches I saw they bore the crest I'd seen on the chests of the gate guards.

I let the path lead me away from them and down to the small glen a mile away from the road. The glen was a sunken meadow through which ran a bubbling creek. The waters fell from a small, steep hill to my left and into a circular pool of water. Above me was the clear night sky, and around me was a quiet serenity.

I collapsed against one of the larger boulders that bordered the water. My feet were glad for a rest. I leaned my back against the hard stone and sighed. My body ached with tension and the exercise. My heart drummed to a quick beat. My drowsiness was surpassed only by my hunger, and I regretted not taking provisions. However, the soft gurgle of the stream calmed my thoughts somewhat, and I closed my eyes. I would take a short nap. Maybe the sun would be up soon and I could escape through the brush.

"What do you mean by this transgression?"

I jumped to my feet and spun around. Across the pond stood the dragon lord, the one to whom I was supposed to belong. His back was concealed in partial shadows, but his eyes glowed with an unnatural green light. They were also narrowed, and at his hip was a sheath and sword. One of his hands lay atop the hilt of the sword.

I snorted. "You're the one who's transgressed. Several kidnapping laws, if I'm not mistaken."

"You cannot escape me. Return with me to the castle at once," he ordered me.

I looked around for a weapon of my own, and snatched a smooth river stone from the ground. I held it up in a throwing position. "Get away! I know how to use this!" I shot back.

I was surprised when his eyes widened. His grip on his sword hilt tightened. "Let down the stone. You don't know what trouble it can cause here."

I scoffed at him. "Like I'm doing that."

His eyes narrowed again and he stepped fully into the light of the night sky. It was my turn for shock as the light revealed a pair of large, red, dragon-like wings at his back. There was the unmistakable canvas-like skin with the thin bones to which they were attached. They were folded behind him, but I could still see that their wingspan must have been enormous.

The dragon lord unsheathed his weapon and made a dash toward the pool. I saw he meant to attack me, so I struck first. I launched the rock at him, but my aim was-well, as reliable as ever. The stone fell short and to the side so that it plopped into the pond near the base of the waterfall.

A gurgling arose from where the stone had dropped in, but it wasn't air escaping. The bubbles continued to rise and flowed over the rest of the pool in a large wave. The dragon lord skidded to a stop a few feet short of the bank and stumbled back. The ground shook in unison with the bubbles. I stumbled backward. My heel tripped on a rock and I fell onto my rear.

A column of water burst from the pond and rose twenty feet into the air. It twisted into a giant spindle shape that spun faster and faster. The width of the column shrunk with each turn, but the width didn't stay consistent. Rather, it took the form of a human.

The excess water drained into the pool, and in a moment what water remained of the tornado burst outward, showering the Lord and me with its wetness. I covered my face with my arm to shield my eyes from the damp, and when I looked at the pool again my jaw dropped open.

There, floating five feet above the surface, was a beautiful woman. She wore a long blue dress that flowed around her like the waves of the ocean. Her skin glistened like white alabaster and was without blemish. Her long, thick hair lay across her shoulders and streamed down her back, and was the dark color of the shallows. The woman's eyes were the color of the clearest waters, and they were focused on me.

When she spoke her voice held an echo like those in seashore caverns. "Why have you transgressed me?"

The dragon lord stepped forward and knelt on one knee. He lay his sword in front of him and bowed his head. "She meant no harm, My Lady. She is ignorant of this world."

The woman half-turned to him, but her eyes remained on me. "Then she is a Maiden." It was a statement rather than a question.

The dragon lord nodded. "Yes, chosen only this evening by me."

A ghost of a smile crossed her lips. "I see. She must be very bold to have escaped the Castle so quickly."

The lord's eyes flickered up to me and he pursed his lips. "Yes, very bold, but I will punish her in a fitting manner."

Anger makes one forget their predicament, and mine was no exception. I jumped to my feet and glared at him. "Like hell you are! I'm not going back there, and you're going to let those other-" My not-so-eloquent speech was interrupted by the twinkling of laughter.

The woman between us tilted her head back and smiled at me. "My my, Dragon Lord, but you have chosen a wild one. She has escaped your castle, eluded your men, violated my waters, and now berates you before me, all in one night."

The lord bowed his head. "I am sorry, My Lady. I swear it will never happen again."

She arched an eyebrow. "It won't? What a pity, for it amuses me." She floated down to my edge of the pond and brought me back to the trouble at hand. I shrank away from her, but her eyes caught mine. Her magnetism was overwhelming. I couldn't retreat. She strode up to me. I shook like a leaf beneath her awesome beauty. "Don't be afraid, little Maiden, for I wish to give you a gift." She cupped my cheek in her palm and smiled at me. Her touch was cold and warm, like the deep and shallow waters of the pool before me. "May your body grow with your love, and let it accept your master in all his forms as your form."

As she spoke her hand glowed with a brilliant blue light. The light soaked into my skin and slipped through my body, leaving me with a warmth like that of a blanket on a cool winter's day. The main focus of the heat lay on the branding on my shoulder, and I swore it soaked into the depths of my skin at that spot.

The woman released me. My shaky legs collapsed so that I sunk onto my knees. She stepped back onto the pond so her bare feet just touched the surface of the water. Small ripples were her only trail as she floated away from me.

She stopped at the center of the pond, and her beautiful smile radiated from her face. "Good luck, little Maiden. Sleep well, my darling."

A cocoon of water slipped upward from the surface of the pond. It enveloped the woman in its wet embrace and retreated back into the water. The woman vanished with the cocoon, and the sight that remained was the astonished look of the dragon lord.

I didn't get to savor his astonishment as a wave of disbelief and fatigue swept over me. That was no mirage of an insane person.

The world spun around me as I clutched my head and swayed from side-to-side. The last I knew was of the dragon lord gliding over the pond toward me and catching me in his strong arms.

CHAPTER 7

I knew nothing else until I awoke some time later beneath the covers of my bed in my new chambers. Sunlight shone through the shut windows and swept over the glistening floor so that it shone back on my eyes. I blinked against the harsh light and sat up. All was quiet and calm except for my buzzing brain.

The woman from the night before. She had been real. There was no way a bunch of medieval maniacs could conjure up something that enchanting. Unless madness was catching.

I had to get out of here.

I flung aside the covers and swung my legs over the side of the bed. That's when I realized I was not in my clothes, but in a flowing white dress. It was of a simple design with a medium-length v-neck collar and no trimmings on the cuffs or hem. The sleeves were long and hung like bells beneath my wrists, and the hem of the dress reached to my ankles. I patted myself, not believing what I was wearing and wondering who had changed me.

Those questions would have to wait. I needed to make my escape before someone noticed I was awake. I hurried across the cold cobble floors to the nearest window and gave a tug on the pane. Nothing. It wouldn't move. The window was shut tight and locked. I frowned and pounded a fist against the wood pane. My reward was a throbbing fist. The wood was as thick as it looked, and twice as strong.

That left the two doors. The side one obviously led to another room which wasn't what I wanted, so I went for the front door. My bare feet pattered on the stones and I wished dearly for my good, solid, warm shoes. I stopped at the entrance and pressed my ear against the wood. Far off were the sounds of chatter and echoing footsteps. Nothing sounded close, so I dared open the door. It, too, wouldn't budge. I was locked in.

The only option left to me was to scream, but first I grabbed a sheet from the bed. Then, positioned by the door, I shrieked like a banshee.

"Is somebody there? Somebody please help me!" I shouted as loud as I could manage. I pounded my fist against the door for added effect. "Help! Somebody help! There's a-um, a badger in here!" Great one, heroine.

Somebody heard my shouts of dangerous badgers because there came the sound of heavy footsteps in the hallway. In a thrice the key was placed in the lock and the door swung open. I jumped forward with the sheet and covered the lead person, who turned out to be the old woman. Behind her was a male servant of the same age along with one of the guards. I was outnumbered, but not outmatched.

"What is this? Stop this at once!" the woman yelped.

She flailed her arms to try to free herself and the men jumped forward to save her and grab me. I pushed the frantic woman into them and they all three fell back in a tangled mass of sheet and limbs. I stepped over them, or rather, on top of them, on my hasty escape from the room.

I skidded to a stop in the hall. Shouts came from my bedroom and down the passage. More heavy feet approached, and what sounded like armor clattering against more metal.

I whipped my head left and right. To my left was the last door along the passage, and the corner that followed the front of the castle. I chose the door and rushed to it. It was unlocked. I dove head-first into the room and shut the door behind me. The footsteps hadn't arrived before I entered the room, nor had the servants and guard managed to free themselves from the blanket. I was safe until they searched the rooms, but perhaps that would give me time to escape from the current room.

In all my frantic rushing and plotting I'd forgotten that the side door to my room opened to this one. I was abruptly reminded when I turned around and found myself staring at the sleeping dragon lord. He lay on a bed much like mine between two large, tall windows. They had shutters to block out the sunlight, but there was enough light streaming between the boards to allow me recognition of his face. I clapped my hands over my mouth to keep from screaming in fright and frustration. Double-whammies that would lead to failure.

CAUGHT BY THE DRAGON

Outside the door the castle servants came alive with their own frustrations. The old woman sternly yelled her orders to others, and footsteps rang through the halls. The sounds of their footsteps came up to my part of the hall and I stumbled away from the entrance. There came the familiar jiggling of a handle as they tried the locked door opposite the one in which I stood.

"Should we check the lord's room?" a man's voice wondered.

"It must be done, but quietly," the old woman replied.

My eyes widened, and I whipped my head to and fro for some place to hide. There was a gap beneath the bed that was large enough to fit an ox. I dove beneath the dangling covers and just slid in my last foot when I heard the door open. Through the sheets I saw a beam of light slip into the room. Light footsteps stepped inside and the door was partially closed. The bed groaned overhead as its occupant did the same.

"What's the meaning of this?" came the Lord's voice.

"I'm sorry to disturb you, My Lord, but the girl has once again escaped," the old woman explained.

"How and when?" came the obvious questions.

"Only a moment ago, and she-well, she threw a blanket over my husband and me," she admitted.

The bed groaned with movement. There was merriment in his tone. "I see. There is no further cause for concern. She is found and that is all that needs be done on your part."

"I'm sorry your assistance was needed, my lord," the woman apologized.

"There is no need. You may leave us." My heart stopped. Us. The dreaded plural.

"Very well."

The footsteps of the other visitors left the room and receded into the distance. Darkness returned to the chamber. I lay perfectly still, not evening daring to breathe. The bed groaned again as a great weight slid from its mattress and stood. I saw the shadow of the lord stride around the bed to the foot.

"Come out where you are hiding beneath the bed," the lord ordered me. I cringed, but remained where I lay. "I know where you are. The mark on your shoulder is more than a sign of your being my possession. It is also an enchantment that allows me to know your location. Also, you are in need of a bath after your hike last night."

At the mention of being a possession I scowled and crawled to the foot of the bed. I stuck my head out to give him the full benefit of my glare. "I am not, nor will I ever be, your-" My breath caught in my throat.

The lord stood naked before me. His body was ripped with pliable muscle, not too hard and not too soft. Just right for a soft porridge of sex. There was also the matter of his member which dangled down, but I guessed would be of some length and thickness when aroused. Somehow the wings were missing.

I let out an 'eep' and slipped back beneath the bed. "P-put some clothes on!" I demanded.

"I do not answer to the whims of my Maiden, now come out from there or I will drag you out myself," he ordered me.

"If you're not getting dressed then I'm not coming out!" I insisted.

"Very well." His shadow slid to the ground and he peeked his head beneath the sheets.

I batted at him with my hands, but he grabbed one of my wrists and pulled me from my hiding place. He pressed my body against his, but I turned my head away from his nakedness. "Let go! Let me go!"

"I will not let you go until you understand your situation," he insisted.

I snorted and whipped my head around to glare into his handsome, albeit evil, face. "You ordered a bunch of thugs to kidnap me from my apartment and bring me to this fantastical world where I would serve you until the end of my days. What exactly am I missing?"

"That you are now a part of this world, and nothing you wish can change that," he told me.

"Wanna try me?" I snapped back.

He pursed his lips and those red eyes of his felt as though they looked into my soul. "You don't understand. The Lady of the Pond granted you a gift, and to leave with the gift would be to put your life in danger."

I froze and felt the color drain from my face. "She did what to me?"

"The Lady has granted you a unique connection to me, and if my enemies were to find out our secret you would be used against me," he rephrased.

My eyebrows crashed down and I tried to wrench myself from his grip, but he was too strong. "What kind of a 'favor' is that? I die if I go home, and staying here means I'm somebody's pawn? Yeah, great favor there."

He pursed his lips. "The Lady's favor is a great blessing, and is rarely given."

I snorted. That was getting to be a habit. "What would be a great blessing is to wake up from this horrible nightmare. Even knowing I had to go back to work would be better than this junk about lords and ladies, and curses and blessings with no benefit and plenty of punishment."

His face softened as he studied mine. "I do not know the precise benefit, but I know I do not wish for you to die."

I paused in my tirade and raised an eyebrow. "Why?"

His manner was quiet and calm, as though he spoke to a wild creature. I must admit I was ready to bolt out the window, even if the drop was a good sixty feet. "While you are my servant, you are also my responsibility and, if fate ordains it, my bride. I would never wish harm to come to you."

I pulled as far away from him as he would allow and scrutinized his handsome features. "I don't believe you."

He raised an eyebrow, and I was surprised when the corners of his lips twitched upward. "Why not? Do you believe me to be some sort of a monster?"

I nodded. "Uh, yeah. You had those wing thingies at that special pond place." I glanced around him, but the wings were still missing. "I don't know where you hid them, but I know they were there." He chuckled and released me from his grasp so he could step back. My eyes inadvertently wandered downward to his member. A blush warmed my cheeks. I spun around and stared at the bed. "Get some clothes on!"

"I would rather you see this without clothes."

My curiosity overcame my shyness, and I peeked over my shoulder at him. He stood with his back toward me and his arms spread apart. My eyes widened as I beheld the pair of leathery wings erupt from him back just below the shoulder blades. The muscles and bones seemed to stretch and pulled themselves from his very skin and form into the dragon-like appendages.

CAUGHT BY THE DRAGON

The whole process took only a few seconds, and he unfurled his wings to their maximum length. His wing tips touched from one end of the long room to the other. He didn't hold the position for long, and retracted his wings so they folded against his back.

It was beautiful, insane, and mind-blowing, all at the same time.

CHAPTER 8

The lord glanced over his shoulder at me. There was a sly smile on his lips. "What do you think?"

"Wow. . ." I murmured. I dared step close enough to stretch out my hands and touched the wings. They felt like stretched skin, and the bones were as hard as any I'd felt, maybe harder. "You're. . .you're really a dragon, aren't you?"

"I consider myself only half dragon. My mother was a Maiden like yourself, and my father took her as his bride," he revealed.

"So you can't go all fire-breathing, scaly dragon-like?" I asked him.

He nodded. "I can, but the transformation is a great strain on my body."

I petted the wing with one hand. It twitched beneath my fingers. "Just. . .just wow. . ." I murmured. The lord shut his eyes and ground his teeth together. His breathing came out in quick gasps, and he appeared in pain. "Are you all right?"

"The wings of a dragon are very sensitive," he informed me.

I yanked my hand away and cringed. "I didn't hurt you, did I?"

"On the contrary. The sensitivity isn't from pain." He half-turned to me and I noticed his member stood erect. "It is a stimulus for mating."

My cheeks resembled the color of a firetruck. I tried to turn away, but the lord caught my chin between the fingers of his hand. He turned my face so I looked into his heated glance. "Do not be afraid. I do not wish to bring you harm."

A strange smell wafted into my nostrils. It was the fragrance of lilacs in spring and of newly cut grass in early summer, my favorite smells. All my fear melted away beneath such comforting scents. The lord wrapped his arms around me, and the smells, too, swirled around me in a soft blanket.

"W-what are you doing to me?" I stuttered. I tried to will myself to hate this creature, this dragon-man who had kidnapped me and made me his slave, but I couldn't. I couldn't do anything but fall into his embrace and soak in the riches of his enticing scent.

"What do you smell?" he whispered into my ear.

"Lilacs, and cut grass," I murmured.

His warm breath ghosted across my tingling flesh. "Beautiful, like you."

I gasped when he pressed a chaste kiss against my neck. "What. . .what's going on? What's happening to me?"

"Ssh. Enjoy the feeling," he whispered. He wrapped his wings around me in a warm embrace, and I felt like a caterpillar preparing for a long, comforting nap before emerging as a beautiful butterfly.

My lord's strong muscles pressed against my pert nipples, and I shuddered at the contact. He pulled my flimsy dress up until the lower hem lay on my hips. One hand held the cloth, and me, in place, and the other slid between my legs. His fingers brushed against the thick, coarse hair and I clutched onto his strong, muscular arms. Like his, my breath quickened.

I closed my eyes and reveled in the feeling of him against me, touching me. My legs shook beneath me as he stroked the sensitive nerves tucked between my hot, wet folds. I clung to him and leaned my cheek against his hard chest. His rapid heartbeat thrilled me. My sensual torture was his.

I yelped as he lifted me into his arms and carried me to the bed. He spread me on the covers and hovered over me. His red eyes burned brightly in the dim light of the room. Sweat glistened over his naked body. I squirmed beneath his hot, intense gaze.

He drew the flimsy gown over my head and flung it aside. I lay naked beneath his eyes. They consumed me like a man starved of food who had finally found his feast. He stretched himself out beside me and explored me with his hands. My flesh tingled beneath his gentle touch. His curious fingers danced across muscle and skin, overlooking nothing of me.

I moaned and squirmed beneath his attentions. My body was on fire. The red-hot heat pooled between my legs. I ached for him, for his hard muscles against me and inside me. His fingers slid down to my wet folds. I groaned as he stroked me again, harder this time and with a faster rhythm.

CAUGHT BY THE DRAGON

My hips rocked with his finger. Sweat soaked my trembling skin. I felt my breasts swell. My hips thickened. Every part of me felt alive with desire for this creature, this man.

His hot breath wafted over my ear, and the thick need in his deep, strained voice sent a thrill of pleasure through me. "Your desire for me is strong, but how badly do you want me?"

I shuddered. My tongue flicked out and whetted my dry lips. "Badly."

"Will you allow me to take you as my own? To make you mine and no other?" he whispered.

His finger moved faster. My muscles began to twitch. Pleasure rippled through me. "Yes. Oh god, yes."

He removed his finger and sat up to look down at me. His lips curled back in a sly grin that revealed his sharp teeth. "Then you will be mine until I release you."

He lay atop me and positioned himself at my wet entrance. I groaned as he effortlessly penetrated me. His thick, throbbing manhood filled me and stroked my bundle of sensual nerves. My body shivered with anticipation. My muscles tensed. I wanted this so badly. More than I'd ever wanted anything else.

My mind and body were enveloped in a haze of lust. I wanted only to pleasure and be pleasured. This man could pleasure me, could take me and claim me again and again. I knew I would enjoy every moment, every thrust, and touch and feel of him against me. Inside of me.

He pulled out and pushed back in. He clenched his teeth, but a hiss escaped his lips. "So. . .tight," he gasped.

I leaned forward and nibbled at his ear. "So wonderful."

He grunted and thrust deeper into me. I lay my head back and moaned. My sultry voice dripped with desire. "Yes. More. So much more."

He wrapped me tight in his arms. His gentle penetrations transformed into wild thrusts. The bed rocked against the wall. I felt my body explode with a deep, blissful pleasure that made me spasm.

My lover continued to thrust, lengthening my bliss for a long minute before he, too, came. He collapsed beside me. One of his wings draped across my naked body and kept the cold from sinking into my sweat.

He pulled me into his arms. Exhaustion swept over me. I closed my eyes and allowed myself to fall into sleep.

CHAPTER 9

I awoke in the deep embrace of both his arms and his wings. I lay on my side, and his warm body pressed against the back of mine. All was quiet, and the darkening shadows in the corners of the room hinted at late afternoon.

I blinked in surprise at my predicament before the memories from earlier surfaced. My perennial blush returned. I tried to pull away from him, but he held me tightly in his arms.

His eyes were closed, but his sleepy voice floated to me. "Where are you trying to run off to, Maiden?"

I bit my lower lip and glanced over my shoulder. "To-um, to the-um, kitchen. I'm kind of hungry." My stomach chimed in with a well-timed growl.

The lord's eyes opened and he smiled at me. "So it seems."

He sat up and his eyes swept over me. I blushed and covered my nakedness with my hands as best I could. He chuckled, and I glared at him. "What's so funny?"

He nodded at my hands. "That you still hide yourself from me after such an intimate act."

My anger flashed through my eyes. "W-well, you did something to me! Those smells of yours made me do it!"

He shook his head. "I did very little. Your own body reacted to the scent from my glands and captured fragrances that you yourself find pleasurable."

I blinked at him. "Your...glands?"

He smiled. "Yes. Dragon males have glands in their wrists and on the sides of their necks that secrete a very fine, invisible mist over potential mates. If the mate is suitable than her mind will create a pleasurable aroma. If the match isn't well-chosen then she will find the scent repugnant."

"So what do the female dragons get?" I asked him.

His eyes wandered down to my breasts. "They have ample assets."

I glared at him. "Not much of a bargain. The guy gets the control and the girl gets a couple of larger jugs."

"Would you rather have our positions the other way around?" he wondered.

I pushed his wings away, but they snapped back like rubber bands. "What I would like is for you to get your wings off me so I can find my clothes and try to escape again."

He sighed and shook his head. "I warned you before that I can find you anywhere in this world. You are no longer hidden from my Second Sight. The Marking ensured that."

"I'm not going to give up. Even if we did have-even if we did do what we did, I still want to go home," I insisted.

CAUGHT BY THE DRAGON

He scrutinized my determined face for a moment and shook his head. "Perhaps I have been too restraining. You seem to be a free soul of sorts. Have you ever hunted on horseback?"

I blinked at him. "No, why?"

A smile slid across his cute lips. "I propose to teach you. One of the others lords has requested me to ride with him today on a hunt, and it would give you a chance to spread your wings. In the figurative sense, that is."

I snorted. "What do you care if I feel trapped?"

"I am not in the habit of keeping prisoners, and a Maiden is the last creature I would wish to imprison. I am too fond of the memories of my mother to dare entrap one who was once in her position," he revealed. He sat up, and his arms and wings released me from the prison. The lord looked straight ahead and pursed his lips. "I wish for your trust, not your fear or anger. I find it vexing at all that I had to choose a Maiden."

I grabbed a sheet from over the side of the bed and covered myself before I sat up. "Then why did you?"

He scoffed. "Custom, and the family bloodline. You view being a Maiden as servitude, but my world sees it very differently. It is an honor to be chosen, and that honor is reserved only for those of your world who are brought through the Portal."

"But why do you need Maidens at all? Why don't you just find a nice girl, settle down, and have cute little dragons?" I persisted.

He shook his head. "It is not that simple. Women are chosen from the other world to reinvigorate the bloodline of the leaders of the dragon clans. This has been a custom for the five large clans for thousands of years."

I wrinkled my nose. "So it's some sort of an honor for people from my world, but not for people from your world?"

The lord nodded. "Yes. The custom is beneficial to the people of my world, and detrimental to your own."

"That's putting it mildly. . ." I muttered. A sudden, horrible thought came to my mind and my heartbeat picked up. "So what happens if the Maiden doesn't get along with the lord? I mean, what happens to the girl? All these Choosings can't work out."

He looked straight ahead and pursed his lips together. "She is allowed to create a new life here, but once she is of this will she will remain within the lord's household. To return to her own world would mean certain death."

I cringed. "So even if I did get away from you I couldn't go home? Ever?"

He turned his head to face me. His dazzling eyes studied me for a long while before he nodded. "I am afraid so. Would it be any different I would still tell you the truth."

I swung my legs over the side of the bed and turned away from him. My shoulders shook. A few loose tears swam in my eyes. "So I'm trapped here. Really, truly trapped here."

He seated himself beside me and laid a hand on my shoulder. "I promise I will make your life here the best I can, whether your chosen as my mate or otherwise."

I whipped my head to him and frowned. "Even if I wanted it, you think it's okay for me to have to jump through all these hoops to be your wife?" I leapt to my feet, taking the blanket with me, and spun around to face him. "You think it's okay to steal me from my home and bring me here-"

"No." He stood and grasped my shoulders. "I do not believe it was right, but what is done is done. Nothing can change that. Nothing can return you to the life you once had." He leaned down so we were face-to-face. "But life does not end. You are a woman of exceptional stubbornness, but in that stubbornness I sense a great strength. I believe you have the strength to be my mate, and I will be much pleased with that."

I turned my head to the side and sniffled. "That's what you say to all the kidnapped girls."

He chuckled. "Only one, and she stands before me." He paused and looked into the distance. A smile teased the corners of his lips. "Or perhaps my three hundred years of life have made me forget the others."

I started back. *"How old are you?"*

The lord grinned and his eyes danced with glee as they looked down at me. "Has no one told you the longevity of dragons? Does your world no longer have stories of them?"

I shook my head. "No. I mean, yeah, it's got stories, but I didn't think they were *real.*"

He opened his wings. The tips scraped against the walls. "Are these not real enough for you?"

My naughty eyes wandered down to his naked torso. *That* was very real. I blushed and averted my eyes from his body. "Y-yes, very real."

He chuckled and out of the corners of my eyes I watched his wings fold. "Perhaps you would be less distracted if I clothed myself. You will catch your death of cold in only that sheet."

I clung the sheet tighter to my body. "I'm fine." A slight chill floated through the window frames. I shuddered.

"I will have Darda bring you your new clothes," he offered.

I glanced at him and frowned. "I'd rather have my old ones."

He shook his head. "They are not suitable for this life."

"I'd still rather have them," I insisted.

The lord sighed, but nodded. "Very well. I will have them returned."

He walked to the head of the bed and pulled on a cord. It must have been the bell to my hunger because my stomach growled again. He chuckled. "And then perhaps we will dine together."

I scoffed. "Do I have a choice?"

The lord walked over to his dresser and pulled a pair of pants on. "There is always starvation."

The door to the chamber opened and the old woman stepped inside. She shut the door behind herself and bowed to us. "You rang, My Lord?"

He gestured to me. "Your Lady wishes to have her old clothes returned, and have breakfast prepared."

She bowed her head. "As you wish. There also came a message for you, My Lord, from Lord Cayden."

The lord arched an eyebrow. "Let me see it." She pulled a small folded note from her pocket and walked over to hand it to him. He unfolded the letter. A smile slipped onto his lips. "Yes. Reply that we will be pleased to have them for breakfast before the ride."

"Yes, My Lord." She left the room.

I glanced at the note he pocketed. My eyes flickered up to his face. "Who are we eating with?"

"The young dragon lord who owes you a great deal of gratitude," he replied as he pulled out a white satin shirt. "Without your interference last night he would not be the joyous man he is this day."

CAUGHT BY THE DRAGON

I blinked at him for a moment before I remembered my 'sacrifice' to Stephanie. "Then he got Stephanie?"

The lord nodded. "Yes, he 'got her,' as you so eloquently put it, and is most pleased with his catch. He is fortunate, as this was his first choosing after becoming the lord of his domains."

I looked the lord up and down. "So are you really three hundred years old?"

He slipped the shirt on and chuckled. "Are you displeased with my aged appearance?"

I snorted. "I've seen teenagers in worse shape, but seriously, how old are you?"

He furrowed his brow as he buttoned his buttons. "I will be three hundred and twenty-eight come this Harvest."

I blinked at him. "Seriously?"

He chuckled. "Very seriously, but I hear the patter of Darda's feet." There was a knock on the door. "Enter."

Darda slipped inside. In her hands was a bundle of my clothes. She walked over and bowed to me. "They have been cleaned for you, My Lady."

I took the pile and looked over my clothes. A washing machine couldn't have done any better. "Thanks."

She bowed again. "I am glad to be of assistance."

My stomach rumbled. The lord chuckled. "Your Lady is curious to know if breakfast ready."

"Yes, My Lord, and Lord Cayden and his Maiden await you," she replied.

He turned to me. "Then dress, My Lady, and we shall feast with friends."

CHAPTER 10

I slipped discretely into my clothes and Darda led the lord and me down the long halls to the ground floor. We passed many other servants of various sizes, and some even of different builds. Swarthy ones with beards and thin ones with pale skin. Some of them wore the green and red colors, others had on clothes that matched those colors of the other dragon lords. All of them stepped aside and bowed their heads to us as we passed.

The main stairs led to a large entrance hall that connected with the castle's interior courtyard. Darda led us left and into a magnificent banquet hall. There were no primitive benches crowded with ruffians. Here there was a single long table with high-backed chairs and elegant curves. The wall opposite the double-doors was covered in tapestries that depicted dragons flying over countrysides. Several of them bore the crests of the various dragon lords.

At the end of the table farthest from the doors sat two familiar faces. One was the pale, young dragon lord, and the other was Stephanie. She turned in her chair and her eyes fell on me. Her face brightened with a smile. She stood and rushed over to me as well as her golden-hemmed white dress would allow.

Stephanie clasped my hands in hers. "Miriam! I'm so glad to see you!"

My dragon lord came up to stand beside me. His eyes twinkled with mischief. "So that is your name."

I glared at him. "You don't have to use it if you don't want to."

He chuckled and bowed his head. "I would be honored."

The slim lord stood and walked over to us to bow his head to my lord. "Thank you for agreeing to-" My dragon lord held up his hand.

"Not so formal this early, Cayden," he pleaded. "I had enough heads bowed to me on the journey to this room to have my fill of formality for another day."

The young lord raised his head and blinked at him. "But My Lord-"

"You have called me that since you were a young hatchling. Now that we are equals I demand you call me Xander," my lord insisted.

I arched an eyebrow. "That's your name?"

He turned to me with a smile. "I won't force you to use it."

"I would be glad to use it," Cayden spoke up.

Xander clapped his hand on Cayden's back and led him toward the end of the table. "Then we shall both be satisfied."

I turned my attention to Stephanie who followed the gold-trimmed lord with a soft gaze. "Has he been treating you well?" I whispered to her.

She started and returned her eyes to me. A blush colored her cheeks and she looked down at the floor. "Really well."

I leaned back and looked her over. "Where are your old clothes?"

"In our-my room," she told me.

I arched an eyebrow and glanced past her at the pair of dragon-men. They were engrossed in their conversation. I looked back to Stephanie and lowered my voice so only she could overhear what I said. "We could try to escape tomorrow morning. They're going to give us horses. We can-" I noticed she bit her lower lip and averted her eyes. I frowned. "What's wrong?"

"I-I-" She took a deep breath and looked me in the eyes. A small smile curled the corners of her lips. "I think he really likes me."

I blinked at her. "What's that got to do-" Her blush darkened. I furrowed my brow. "Are you. . .do *you* want to stay here?"

She cringed, but gave a weak nod. "Yes. I mean, he said I couldn't go home. Some portal thing won't let us."

I dropped my hands off her shoulders and pursed my lips. "I. . .I guess you're right."

Her face fell. She set a hand on one of my shoulders. "I'm sorry, Miriam. I didn't mean-"

"We would be honored if you ladies would join us for breakfast," Xander spoke up.

I frowned and glanced at the windows between the tapestries. Their foggy glass revealed the late afternoon sun outside the castle walls. "But it's almost night," I pointed out.

Xander chuckled as he pulled out a chair to the left of the head of the table. "Yes, but the Choosing is a special time for we dragon lords. Therefore, we celebrate our gathering all through the night and rest during the day."

I arched an eyebrow. "So is this some sort of a frat party?"

The dragon lord shook his head. "I'm afraid I'm not familiar with that term."

I sighed. "It's where guys get together and prove how manly they are by drinking and eating a lot."

Xander nodded. "Then this is similar to a 'frat party,' as you call it. But enough of talk. There is a feast before us that begs to be consumed."

I took my seat on his left with Cayden and Stephanie opposite me, and Xander at the head. A feast of meat and mead was set before us, and I must admit I did justice to everything within reach.

Xander speared a slice of duck with his fork and glanced at Cayden. "Where shall we take our ride this evening? In the direction of Bruin Bay, or shall we head to the Coven Caves for a fine hunt there?"

Cayden choked on the mead he just swallowed. He coughed and patted his chest with his fist as his wide eyes stared at the dragon lord. "So far, My-" Xander gave him a warning look, "-must we travel so far, Xander?"

"Why not?"

Cayden glanced nervously at Stephanie. "This is my first ride. I am not sure how far I can-"

"True. I do see your concern," Xander replied. He leaned back and took a bite of the hunk of meat. "Perhaps a closer point on the map, or around the castle grounds. They are quite-"

"I'd like to see this Portal," I spoke up.

Cayden's face paled. Stephanie blinked at me.

Xander sat up and raised an eyebrow. "Why would you wish to see that?"

I shrugged. "For some closure."

Cayden glanced at my dragon lord and pursed his lips. "I think maybe we should call-" Xander raised his hand and silenced the younger lord.

Xander dropped his hand and shook his head. "No. Closure is important, but-" he looked into my eyes, "-there may be pain."

"I'll live with it," I assured him.

Xander bowed his head and stood. "Then I suggest we set off before darkness spoils the view for our Maidens."

We left the dining hall, but turned right in the entrance hall and walked to the back of the castle where a small wooden door led us out onto the green lawn. The bottom of the setting sun skiffed the horizon in the far west and long shadows stretched out from the forest over the lawn.

The animals in the nearby pastures crowded the fences and trampled dirty straw beneath their hooves. One of the species was a full-coated sheep with curved horns. A wide smile spread across Stephanie's face as she glimpsed a few lambs among the two dozen adults.

"How adorable!" she squealed before she hurried to them.

CAUGHT BY THE DRAGON

"Wait!" Cayden yelled. He ran after her and grabbed her wrist before she reached the fence. "Do not approach them!"

She looked over her shoulder and blinked at him. "But why?"

He released her and picked up a stick. "This is why."

Cayden tossed the stick into the mess of wool. The sheep let out a terrible wail of a bleat and lunged at the stick. They beat the wood with their hooves and rammed it with their heads. The stick was smashed and trampled to broken bits.

Stephanie gasped and stumbled back. "My god. . ."

I looked to Xander and jerked my head in the direction of the woody carnage. "What kind of mutton are you raising?"

"Not all that resembles creatures in your world are the same in ours," Xander schooled us. He nodded at the creatures as they strolled away from the fence. "These creatures may have wandered into our world long ago and changed their appearance, or perhaps they were changed in your world and what we see are the originals. Either way, caution is the best course of action in dealing with our plants and animals."

Cayden grasped Stephanie's shaking shoulders and looked to us. "Perhaps we should postpone the ride."

Xander shook his head. "No. My Maiden's curiosity will not be satisfied until she has seen the Portal."

"Damn right," I spoke up. I glanced around. "Where are the horses?"

Cayden blinked at me. "Horses?"

I narrowed my eyes and nodded. "Yeah. This is supposed to be a-aah!" Xander swept me into his arms.

A sly smile covered his lips as he looked down at me. "Your escape has taught me one important lesson. You are not afraid of heights."

I glared at him. "What's that got to do with anything? And why aren't you putting me-" His wings burst from his back and stretched across the open plain. The scales shimmered in the glistening sun.

"You may wrap your arms around my neck, but not too tightly," he told me.

I frowned. "Why would I-" He beat his wings and we were propelled off the ground.

The sharp blades turned to seas of green as we quickly left the earth below us. Every flap of his powerful wings lifted us ten feet.

I looked down at the ground a hundred feet below us and yelped. My arms instinctively wrapped around his neck and I quivered against his warm chest. We reached an altitude double that and hovered in place as his wings gently flapped.

"How are you enjoying the ride?" he asked me.

I whipped my head up and glared at him. "You said there'd be horses!"

He shook his head. "No, I asked if you had ridden a horse. This is much the same."

"No, it's not!"

Xander nodded his head at the forest in front of us. Through some fifteen miles of winding roads was a meadow. "The Portal lies there. Do you still wish to see it?"

"More than ever," I growled.

CAUGHT BY THE DRAGON

Cayden with Stephanie in his arms joined us. She quivered harder than me, but her driver didn't seem to mind her clinging to him so closely. "Are we ready?" the young lord wondered.

Xander nodded. "Yes. Let us go."

CHAPTER 11

Xander angled his legs behind him and his head forward. His wings flapped hard and we were pushed forward by the momentum. We sped past the ground beneath us. A cool wind whipped my face. I shivered and turned away to face away and toward his chest.

"Cold?" he asked me.

I gave him the Evil Eye. "What do you think?"

"That you are not enjoying the ride as much as I would wish," he commented.

I glanced down at the earth far below us. "You don't exactly come with a seat belt or parachute."

He blinked at me. "Seat belt?"

I shook my head. "Never mind. Just don't drop me."

He chuckled. "I believe I can agree to your request."

CAUGHT BY THE DRAGON

We flew over the thick forests of tall, ancient trees. Our shadows ghosted over the needled tops as the sun set to our right. A cool wind whipped my hair over my face and over my bare arms. The warmth of the dragon lord's body stifled some of my shivering.

The winding gravel road traveled with us. I looked ahead at its future. The road ended at a small village of thatched-roof houses. Smoke floated from the chimneys and dim light of candles.

The exception to the stillness lay at the southern-most edge of the clump of houses. There, in a round clearing that stretched into the trees, arose a large, twenty-foot tall upright hoop made of stone and vines. The hoop stood at the extreme end of a stone platform. On the ground in front of the platform was a round stone alter like a bird-feeder, but filled with oil. A fire three feet tall fed off the flammable liquid and pierced the air with its twisting flames.

The platform was reached by six wide steps. Two figures clothed in cloaks of brown and black stood on the platform on either side of the steps. Three others stood around the tall alter of fire. They were clothed in cloth of gold, green and blue, and white. All of their cloaks had large slits in the backs, but their underclothing and skin were hidden by multiple layers of clothing.

Around them were a half-dozen others cloaked in gray habits that had no hoods. Those men were all around thirty and their hair was cut short in the bowl look. The monk-like men poured the oil into the hungry fire, swept the ground around the alter, or stood off to one side in a line.

The cloaked group looked up at us as we landed. Xander and Cayden set us down as the three figures around the fire came over to us. They bowed, and the one in green and blue stepped forward.

"My Lords, you do us a great honor with your visit," he greeted us.

Xander smiled and bowed his head in return. "It is too often we forget to pay our respects to you who guard the Portal."

The person removed his hood and revealed himself as a man of fifty. His gray-stranded hair flowed down his back in a tail. Wrinkles teased the corners of his eyes, and there was a soft smile on his face. "It is, and always will be, an honor to manage the Portal for you, My Lord. How may we serve you this night?"

Xander gestured to me. "My Maiden wishes to see the Portal in all its mythical glory."

The man bowed his head. "As you wish it, My Lord, but I cannot perform the ritual on my own."

Xander smiled. "One must admire your diligence to code, Apuleius." He looked to Cayden who stood beside us. "Cayden, does my priest have your permission to open the Portal?"

Cayden nodded. "I will allow my priest to help."

The man in the golden cloak removed his hood. He was about seventy with more wrinkles than an unsettled pond. His soft blue eyes smiled at Stephanie. "I will gladly do My Lord's bidding, but would also congratulate you on a beautiful Maiden. I have not seen the likes of her in many years." Stephanie blushed and looked at the ground.

Cayden bowed. "Thank you, Jethro. I, too, am most pleased with her."

"But to the reason for our visit," Xander reminded them.

CAUGHT BY THE DRAGON

Apuleius nodded. "Yes, My Lord. Your will shall be done."

Apuleius and Jethro walked up the stone steps to stand ten feet from the tall hoop. Each of them held up an opposite arm, one left and one right, and closed their eyes. Their lips moved, but no sound reached my ears.

Something shifted on the Portal, though. The vines that covered the archway drew back and revealed a set of six carved figures. They were standing dragons, and were so intricate I could see their scales. There were two sets of three, one on each side of the arch and they faced the top center. In the center was a small drop of water.

The drop of water glowed blue, and the dragons glowed the respective colors of the five houses with the addition of a red dragon at the top left. Opposite that one was a green dragon. The brilliance from the carved figures flowed over the arch and into the hole. It spread over the interior like a thin film of rippling water. The film covered the center of the archway to the surface of the platform.

An explosion of light burst from the center and spread outward to the stone arch. The burst left behind a smooth, reflective surface that revealed my astonished face.

Xander picked up a small pebble from the swept ground and offered me his arm. "Shall we?"

In my stupor I took his arm and let him lead me up the stairs. Cayden and Stephanie followed behind us. We stopped where the priest stood. The pair stepped aside and let us stand in front of the water portal.

Xander swept his eyes over the surface. "Quite impressive, is it not? It took a century of ancient magic from the ruling houses of the dragons to bring this to fruition.

The stone figures were carved by the dragons themselves and infused with their life forces."

"Did it hurt them?" Stephanie wondered.

Xander shook his head. "No, but it left them and their lines spiritually weakened."

I arched an eyebrow. "Than why did they do it?"

He looked down to study me. "Because they believed the reward was worth the price. The Maidens would offer a rejuvenation of their line, a new promise to their descendants."

Something on the ground caught my attention. I stooped and picked it up to turn it in my fingers. It was a bit of compressed clay dropped from the tire of the pig-men's truck.

I held it up so Xander could see it. My lips pursed together as my eyes flickered to him. "So how were those pig-men able to go through?" I questioned him.

"Their kind are the exception to the rule. They are not of our world, nor nor yours, but between them as travelers," he explained.

I let the dirt clod fall to the ground. It crumbled to dust. I glanced at the portal. "I see."

Xander frowned. He picked up a rock from the ground and walked up the stairs. The men in cloaks bowed their heads and stepped aside. He threw the rock underhanded at the gray blob. The hard matter hit the gooey center. There was a small flash of light at the point of contact. I saw the rock burst into a thousand tiny, colorful fragments of glass. The fragments fell to the ground in front of the portal.

Xander half-turned to me and gestured to the remains of the stone. "That is what happens to anything from our world, of which you are now a part."

CAUGHT BY THE DRAGON

My heart sank as that last bit of hope inside me died. Stephanie set her hand on my shoulder and gave me a squeeze. "I'm sorry," she whispered.

I gave her a bitter smile and shrugged. "I was just-"

"Dragons!" someone yelled.

We turned to one of the gray monks. He pointed at the sky, and we followed his direction. Six large forms flew through the sky. These were the true dragons, those of myth and legend. The entire length of their bodies from nose to long, whipping tail was fifty feet. The wide span of their leathery wings carried a great weight of claws as sharp as knives and scales as hard as steel. Their long heads ended in mouths full of razor-sharp teeth. Four thick, stubby legs were tucked against their scaled bellies. The end of those legs held long claws covered in silver talons forged by man.

One of the gray monks staggered back and tripped over his own feet. He fell onto his rear and gaped up at the sky with wide, terror-filled eyes. "The Bestia Draconis!"

Xander hurried over and stood between me and the shadows. His green eyes flashed and his lips curled back in a snarl.

Cayden grabbed Stephanie likewise. The young dragon lord looked to his elder. "How can they be this far from the coast without our knowing?"

Xander's eyes never left the shadows in the skies as he shook his head. "I cannot understand it, but we shall make them regret this intrusion."

His hands on my shoulders lengthened into sharp claws. He pulled me to the side and Cayden did the same with Stephanie so we stood shoulder-to-shoulder. Xander turned to me and grasped my shoulders as he looked me in the eyes.

"Remain here."

I frowned. "But what are you going to do?"

"I will fight them, but you can do nothing against these fiends," he insisted.

I shook my head. "What can you do-"

"Promise me you will remain here." I pursed my lips, but nodded. He smiled. "Then wait for me. I will return."

Xander stepped backward and off the platform. He spread his wings out on either side of him. My mouth dropped open as I watched his skin thicken with scales. A tail burst out from his back and stretched itself onto the ground. His limbs stretched and twisted into four thick legs. He settled onto his four legs as the rest of his body transformed into monstrous shape of a huge green dragon. The handsome face vanished into the lengthened mug of the beast.

He whipped his head up and snarled at the red forms that flew over the clearing. His wings flapped and took him airborne. Cayden reluctantly separated himself from Stephanie and took Xander's empty place. He, too, transformed into a majestic dragon, but a smaller one with golden scales. He sailed into the sky after Xander.

Four of the dragons broke off and headed for Xander and Cayden. They collided in a vicious battle of teeth and claws. Cayden dodged a double attack on his wings and flew around the enemy dragons to attack them from behind.

Xander just rammed through his foes, tearing and snapping at their wings and bodies. One of them let out a terrible screech and fell to the ground. The earth shook as it struck the dirt near the platform. Stephanie cried out and clung to me. I watched in a stupor as the dragon's body shrank to that of a naked man. He lay face-down and blood pooled beneath him from wounds that matched the damage on his previous form.

The other two dragons swung around the battle and aimed downward at the platform. The five wizards raised their hands and chanted phrases I wouldn't have understood even if I could have heard all the words above the screeches of the dragons. Light respective of their cloaks burst from their hands and flew up at the dragons.

One was hit, but the other did a barrel roll and dodged the attacks. The unscathed dragon swooped down and grabbed one of the gray-cloaked men. He flailed in its grasp as it flew to the portal and released him.

Stephanie and I ducked as he flew past. The man collided with the Portal and let out a horrible scream before he burst into dust. The injured dragon dropped to the ground, but landed on all fours. It swung its tail in a full circle and knocked away all the men in robes, the colorful ones included.

Its red eyes fell on Stephanie and me. The creature curled its lips back in a snarl as it marched toward us. Its silver talons clinked as it walked onto the stone platform.

I shoved Stephanie to our right. "Run!"

She stumbled in that direction as the dragon let out a screech. It opened its wings and threw itself at us. Stephanie fell off the platform, but the dragon cut me off with its long neck and wide body. It lowered its head and hissed at me.

I held up my hands and backed up toward the Portal. "Can't we talk about this?"

The creature roared and lunged at me. That's when a dark shadow fell from the sky and landed atop it. It was the green dragon. *My* dragon. Xander clamped his jaws onto his foe's neck. The dragon screamed and flailed, sending its tail and wings thrashing about.

I stumbled back and my heels tripped on one of the stones. My arms flailed at my sides to stop me, but gravity took hold.

Xander turned around. His green eyes widened. He leapt off the dragon and toward me. He stretched his neck out as I stretched my hand. Our flesh grazed each other and then fell away. The last I saw was the dragon beneath Xander lifting one of its silver-taloned feet to strike him.

A moment later I felt a warm pool of liquid wrap around me like a spongy blanket. The world of dragons was blotted out by a world of warped gray liquid. It pressed all around me. I couldn't breathe. My vision began to blur.

Just as I thought I would pass out the suffocating world around me opened up. I dropped back-first out of the vortex and landed hard on the ground. What little air was left in me was knocked out in a short wheeze. As I lay there trying to suck in air the portal in front of me shrank to nothing.

I had ample time to study the black sea of twinkling stars that was above me. Electrical wires and poles cut the sky into squares. The far-off sounds of traffic came to my ears. I sat up on my shaky arms and looked around. My eyes widened.

I was home.

CHAPTER 12

I was also in the city dump. The heaps of trash and tall piles of rusted cars glared down at me like giant shadows of ancient creatures. I'd had enough of those for a lifetime.

I scrambled to my feet and fled as fast as my shaky legs could manage. My feet pounded against the hard-packed dirt as my mind whirled with frantic thoughts of what I should do. I couldn't go back to my apartment. The pig-men knew where I lived. Blake also knew where I worked.

That meant there was only one place to hide. That is, if Blake hadn't found out her address, too.

I managed to stumble my way down twelve blocks to an old apartment building in the artistic part of town. Whether wanted or not, murals adorned the sides of the buildings and the streetlight posts. Trees were randomly planted in holes that littered the sidewalks. Signs outside the bottom floors of apartment buildings advertised everything from palm reading to palm trees.

I stopped in front of an old four-story brick apartment building. Each floor was let out to a single person. I was glad to see the lights were on on the third floor. I hurried up the stoop to the front door. To the left were four buzzers, and beside each button was a nameplate.

I pressed the buzzer for the third floor. A sniffling voice answered. "Hello?"

My heart nearly burst from hearing that familiar voice. "Heth! You gotta let me in!"

"Miriam! Is that really you?"

A noise behind me caught my attention. I glanced over my shoulder. The street was deserted. "It won't be only me for long if you don't open the door!"

"Sure! Just wait a sec!"

I heard her fumble for something and curse. A buzzer rang to my right. That signaled the door was unlocked. I opened the door and sidled inside. The door clicked shut behind me. All was quiet in the small entrance hall for two seconds. Then the pounding of footsteps rang down the stairs in front of me.

Heather flew around the last landing on the stairs and swooped down upon me. She flung her arms around me and took the brunt of the blow as I crashed into the wall near the door.

"You're safe! Oh my god, you're safe!" she cried.

I pried her off me and smiled into her tear-soaked face. "Yeah, but remind me never to look for a man again."

She sniffled. Her lower lip quivered. "It's because of me, isn't it? I told you to get a guy and when you tried on your own a guy got you, didn't he?"

I snorted. "Let's just say I was dragged into the wrong crowd, but I'll tell you everything in your apartment."

She grabbed my hand and pulled me toward the stairs. "Yeah. We'll make it a girl's night out."

Heather dragged me up to her apartment and plopped me in one of the chairs at her dining table. The floor apartments were fully furnished with antique furniture and my friend's own strange taste for lava lamps. The place was alive with the floating blobs of colorful goop.

I leaned back and sighed. The old smell of the industrial, human world was wonderful to behold.

Heather sat opposite me. She looked over my clean but disheveled clothes. "You don't look like you've been kidnapped for a few days."

A small smile slipped onto my lips. "I'm not sure you're going to believe what I'm going to tell you."

"Try me."

So I tried her. When I was done with my tale Heather lay her arms on the table and leaned toward me. She studied me with a hard eye. "Are you trying to pull my tail?"

I shook my head. "I've had enough of tails, thanks. Besides, everything I told you is true."

"If it's true show me the mark. The one on the shoulder," she challenged me.

I grabbed my shirt and tugged it down my arm. There, in all its green glory, was the mark of Xander's house.

And it suddenly hurt like hell.

I cried out and grabbed my shoulder. The pain was like a hot poker against my skin. A faint green glow was visible between my fingers. I clenched my teeth and doubled over.

Heather jumped to her feet and raced to my side. "What is it? What's wrong?"

"Burning," I ground out.

"L-lemme get an ice pack!" she suggested.

She raced to the kitchen. I shut my eyes and tried to block out some of the pain. A startling image of Xander in a bed came to my mind's eye. He was covered in sweat. A crowd stood around him with Darda and Cayden among them. Their faces looked grave. I gasped and my eyes flew open. The vision vanished.

Heather returned with a bunch of ice stuffed into a plastic sandwich bag. She yanked my hand away and slapped it on my burning skin. I yelped at the opposing sensations as they clashed on my flesh.

My friend cringed. "Sorry!"

I clutched the bag to myself and shook my head. "Just shut up for a sec."

For once Heather listened to me. She stood there in silence as the pain ebbed and flowed, driving me to clench and unclench my teeth. After a long five minutes the pain faded. My body relaxed. I let my shoulders slump as I removed the thawed ice pack from my arm.

Heather took it in her hands and bit her lip as she studied me. Her body shivered. I sighed and nodded. "You can speak again."

Out spilled all the words she'd kept inside her those long minutes. "Areyouokay? Whatthehellwasthat? Istheresomethingwrongwiththedragon? Canyousensehisfeelings? Howbaddidithurt?"

I held up one hand and massaged my temple with the other. "I'm all right, and yeah, it hurt like hell, but I don't know why."

She furrowed her brow and rubbed her chin between her pointer finger and thumb. "Maybe it has something to do with your dragon husband."

I whipped my head up and frowned at her. "He's not my husband."

She dropped her hand and shrugged. "It kind of sounds like you were married to him, and you two did-well, *everything*. Even the honeymoon night."

"He kidnapped me and seduced me. That's it," I insisted. I sighed and pinched the bridge of my nose. "I could really go for a drink. . ."

Heather grinned. "Hard or knock-you-off-your-feet?"

My eyes flickered up to her. "Got any wipe-the-hard-drive-clean?"

She nodded. "Yep, but I warn you it tastes like socks and cough syrup."

"Then I'll take it."

She walked over to the connected kitchen and wrangled about for some glasses and a bottle of what appeared to be tar. "I still think that burning's got something to do with-well, you-know-who."

I slumped in my chair. "Maybe, but I-well, it doesn't concern me."

Heather paused and glanced over her shoulder. A sly smile slipped onto her lips. "You sure?"

I frowned. "What's that supposed to mean?"

She looked back at the glasses and shrugged. "Oh, I was just thinking you might-you know, kind of like him."

I rolled my eyes. "Are you seriously trying to set me up with a dragon?"

"He's probably got great teeth," she pointed out.

I snorted. "Yeah, he flosses the whole lamb out of them every day."

She whipped her head over her shoulder to look at me. "Really?"

"I was joking." Another sharp pain hit me in the shoulder. The agony only lasted a few seconds and felt more distant than before, like the connection was weaker. I lay my hand over my mark and recalled the last memory I had of that world. That red dragon was aiming those silver talons at Xander.

"Do you know if silver hurts dragons?" I asked my friend.

Heather raised her eyes and furrowed her brow. "I never heard that it could, but I never heard of dragons turning into cute guys, either." She glanced over her shoulder at me. "Why?"

I stared at the floor and shook my head. "It's nothing."

Heather walked over to the column that made up one end of the bar that separated the kitchen from the dining area. She leaned her shoulder on the column and crossed her arms over her chest. "What is it?"

I raised my eyes and glared at her. "I said it was nothing."

She held up her hands and retreated into the kitchen. "All right, all right. Sheesh."

I rubbed my aching shoulder and bit my lower lip. That last memory wouldn't leave me. A knot gathered in my stomach.

"What the hell happened?" I whispered.

"Why should you care?" Heather called from the kitchen. She picked up our glasses and carried them to the table. "I mean, it's not like you love the guy, right?"

I blushed and averted her eyes as she plopped one of the mugs down in front of me.. "I didn't say anything."

She sat down in the chair beside me and snorted. "Yeah, and I'm a nun who's taken a vow of silence. Now come on, what's *really* bothering you?"

"I said it's nothing."

She leaned close to me and studied my face. "Are you blushing?"

I cringed and turned my face away. "I'm not blushing."

A gleeful smile spread across her lips. "You *do* like him, don't you? You've fallen for your knight in green scales!"

I whipped my head back and glared at her. "How could I even like him? He had me kidnapped so he could keep up some kind of-" Heather let out a squeal as she plopped herself in the chair beside me.

"You wouldn't be complaining about him if you didn't like him so much!" she insisted.

I blinked at her. "Are you *nuts*? I could never-" Another white-hot pain hit me in the shoulder. I winced and clapped my hand over the tattoo.

Heather sighed and shook her head. "You gotta get past the Denial stage and take a shortcut to the Acceptance one."

"I'm not grieving!" I snapped.

She nodded at my shoulder. "But I bet you're going to be if you don't find out what's wrong over there. I bet that tattoo has something to do with your connection with him, and if it's hurting that might mean he's hurting, too."

"Are you even listening to me?"

"You said there was a big battle when you got pushed into the portal? Maybe he's seriously injured, or maybe he's dying."

Her words made me freeze. My blood ran cold as my heart skipped a couple of beats. The last image of that attacking dragon, the pain in my arm, the vision I just experienced. None of them pointed to a happy and healthy dragon lord.

Heather's soft, low voice broke through my reverie. "Well?"

I lifted my eyes and blinked at her. "Well what?"

She rolled her eyes. "Are you going to get back there or do I have to carry you?"

I started back. "Are you nuts? I'm not going back there!"

She jumped to her feet and grabbed my hand. "Come on. Let's get you going back to your scaly soul-mate before he dies or eats someone or something."

Heather dragged me out of my chair and toward the door. "Wait! Wait a minute!" I yanked my hand free from her grasp and stumbled back to my place at the table. I glared at my 'friend.' "Are you trying to get me killed? That other dragon wasn't trying to hug me before I dropped through that portal that also tried to kill me!"

She put her hands on her hips and tapped her foot on the floor. "Miriam, you've got the best chance in your life to save a strong, handsome man who loves you, and here you are standing there like you don't love him yourself."

"How can I?" I argued.

Heather smiled and stepped forward. She dropped a hand on my shoulder and looked me in the eyes. "Stockholm Syndrome." My face fell. She laughed and patted my shoulder. "Because sometimes love starts under strange circumstances. Besides, could you really live with yourself if he died?"

I pursed my lips. She had me there. Heather slipped around me and pressed her palms against my back so she could steer me toward the door. "Come on. Let's go save your scaly boyfriend."

CHAPTER 13

    I reluctantly let her drive me back to the junk yard and I led her to the specific area where the portal disappeared. We stopped near one of the larger trash piles.

    I turned to her and folded my arms. "It's supposed to be here, but I don't know if love is going to get that thing to open."

    Heather cupped her chin in one hand and furrowed her brow. "Do you remember how you got in the first time?"

    I rolled my eyes. "No. I forgot to click on my internal video recorder before they knocked me out."

    She strolled around the area looking at the ground and up in the air. "Maybe there's a button or something."

    I ran a hand through my hair and sighed. "Or maybe we're not going to get this thing open and we should just go home."

CAUGHT BY THE DRAGON

Heather stomped up to me and grabbed my hands. She looked me in the eyes and frowned. "Don't you dare give up on me and your heart this fast. We're counting on you."

I snorted. "When did my heart get a vote on this?"

"When I said it had one."

"And does my heart have any ideas how to get this portal thing open?"

Heather paused. Her eyes widened and her wild grin stretched across her face. "Maybe that's it!"

I leaned back and frowned. "Maybe what's it?"

She dragged me to my butt-mark in the dirt and arranged us so we faced each other. "Maybe with your love and your mark thingy you can open the portal. They're both from the other world, right?"

I blinked at her. "I have no idea how that would work."

She shrugged. "Neither do I, but there's got to be a way. Maybe you could slap your mark or kiss it or do something."

My face fell. "Seriously?"

She released my hands and stepped to the side where she crossed her arms. "It's all up to you now, Miriam. I got you here, now you've got to get that mark going."

"All you did was drive me here!" I argued.

"Close enough, now focus on that mark!"

I sighed and glanced down at my shoulder. There was a dull pain from that spot that made my whole arm ache. I pulled up my sleeves and grasped my mark in my hand. The skin felt warm. It reminded me of his body against mine, and the warmth in his eyes. I thought of my vision, and the last memory I had of him.

I closed my eyes and pressed my lips together. My whispered words floated through the quiet air. "Damn it. . .why'd you have to go and be a hero?"

The pain in my shoulder increased ten-fold. My eyes flew open and I whipped my head to my shoulder. The lines of the mark glowed a bright green and my hand glowed a bright blue. The brilliant colors twined together like silk bands. They floated into the air and swept in front of me. The pair of bands parted and drew two halves of a circle in the air before me.

The border of the portal materialized. The two bands finished their work with a bang as the center darkness blew into existence. I stumbled back and stared blankly at the complete Portal.

Heather rushed to my side and steadied me. Her wide eyes stared at the reflective surface. "Wow." She looked at me. "How'd you do that?"

I dropped my hand and shook my head. "I don't know."

She stepped forward and looked at me before she jerked her head toward the portal. "Well? What are you waiting for?" I smiled and gave her a tight hug. We parted and I could see a few tears in her eyes. "Go on. You shouldn't keep a dragon waiting. He might eat you."

I rolled my eyes. "Thanks. That really helps."

She grinned. "I'll always be there to give you the good news, now get going."

Heather stepped aside. I looked to the Portal and took a deep breath knowing I'd need it.

With a hope and a prayer I leapt into the void. The trip was exactly like the first one, but the exit was a little different. I stumbled out of the other side of the portal and onto the hard stone platform. The front of my foot betrayed me this time and I tripped on one of those rocks. I fell onto my hands and knees.

A green cloak came into my limited view. I tilted my head up and into the shocked face of the ancient sage. Behind him were his peers. Their faces had the same astonished expression.

I grinned up at them. "Um, hi. You don't happen to-" My eyes noticed a large stain over the stones. The stain was a distinct red color. My heart quickened. I looked up at them. "Where's Xander?"

Apuleius knelt down and offered me his hand. "We must get you to him immediately."

That didn't do a thing to stop my fast-beating heart. I took his hand and he helped me up. Apuleius turned to one of the gray-cloaked men. "I will escort My Lady to My Lord."

The gray cloaked man whipped his head up so quickly his hood fell backward to reveal his astonished face. "But Father Apuleius-"

"If anyone is to see My Lord to health, it shall be his Lady," Apuleius told him. He glanced at the others and bowed his head. "Please forgive me-" The one in the gold cloak raised his hand and shook his head.

"Do not concern yourself with apologies. We all would risk our cloaks for our lords." He smiled and nodded at the air above us. "Now to the skies before I throw you myself."

Apuleius returned the smile. "Thank you, old friend." He turned to me. "If you would climb on my back, My Lady."

I blinked at him and glanced at his back. "I don't think I'd-"

My mistake was cut short when the slits in the back of his cloak parted to make room for his large green dragon wings.

"If you will pardon my forwardness, My Lady," he apologized.

I didn't have time to ask him why before he swept me into his arms. He flapped his wings and we were airborne. Like any unprofessional rider I clung tightly to his neck and prayed.

I was up to bartering my soul for a reprieve from the wind whipping through my hair when we reached the castle. The long fifteen miles had been covered in a little under fifteen minutes. An eternity for my heart, and I hoped I wouldn't expect to find Xander in an eternity of sleep.

The guards greeted us with spears as Apuleius landed in the courtyard. I slid out of his arms and stumbled forward. My legs shook so bad I leaned on the old sage for support. His wings shrank until his old frame returned to his complete human form. It was only then that the guards lowered their spears.

Apuleius looked to one of the green-clothed guards. "Does Our Lord still live?"

He pursed his lips, but nodded. "Yes, Priest Apuleius, but only just barely."

Apuleius turned to me and pressed his hand against my back. "If you would follow me, My Lady."

He led me through the maze of corridors and doors to Xander's chambers. We found two green-clothed guards on either side of the door. They bowed their heads and one of them opened the door for Apuleius and me. I wondered how many doors were shut to this priestly fellow.

CAUGHT BY THE DRAGON

That is, until I saw the figure in the bed. All thought fled from my mind. I froze just inside the doorway. There, beneath many layers of blankets, lay Xander. His face was ashen and sweat covered his brow. Bandages criss-crossed his chest. He shivered and clenched his teeth. Near the foot of the bed stood Cayden, and at his side was Stephanie. Darda stood behind them with her husband.

Apuleius hurried to his side. He looked from Xander's pale face to a man who stood on the opposite side of the bed. He was a white-haired, gray-bearded gentleman in a long shirt with sleeves and leggings. His hands were covered in silk gloves that were stained by chemicals and sweat. His face was grave.

"How is his health?" Apuleius asked him.

The doctor pursed his lips. He closed his eyes and shook his head. "There is nothing more my skills can do."

I hurried over to Apuleius's side and set my hands on the covers. A closer look at Xander's face didn't help the heavy feeling in my heart. His breathing was quick and each breath was a struggle.

I looked at all the faces of those who surrounded me. "What's wrong with him?"

"The Bestia Draconis wore poison-tipped silver talons. One of them cut Xander very deeply," Cayden explained.

I felt the color drain from my face. The ache in my shoulder got worse as I looked around at the dire faces. "Isn't there an antidote?"

The doctor closed his eyes and shook his head. "My abilities are beyond this poison. Only the tears given by the Lady of the Pond can heal such a poison."

I furrowed my brow. "The woman who lives in the pond near the castle? What's so hard about that?"

Cayden sighed. "The Lady only appears to those whom she deems worthy of her attention. In this instance, she would not heed our calls and appear to us."

I pursed my lips and spun on my heels so I faced the doorway. "Then I'll go," I announced as I marched toward the door.

The guards on either side stepped in my way. I whipped my head over my shoulder to look at Cayden. "If you want that dragon lord to make it then let me go."

Cayden shook his head. "We cannot allow you to escape again."

I glared at him and pointed a finger at Xander. "Do you want him to die?"

"If you were to-"

"Let her go." The words came from Darda. She looked up at Cayden and met his gaze. "My Lord would wish it so."

Cayden sighed, but nodded his head. He turned his attention to the soldiers. "Step aside, and I will go with you."

The guards stepped aside. I hurried to the door and grabbed the knob, but paused and looked over my shoulder. I gave the group a smile and a thumbs up. "I'll be right back."

CHAPTER 14

I had no plan, though at that point what I really wanted was a machete and a flashlight. The world of dragons was very dark. The only light I had was the moon in the sky. I fumbled my way through the woods with Cayden as my guide. Every rock and tree branch tried to murder me, but the sound of the waterfall kept hope alive within me.

Cayden held open the last homicidal branch as I stumbled into the clearing. The gurgling brook greeted us with its soft sounds, and the falling water glistened in the moonlight as its sparkling droplets splashed over the rocks.

Cayden stepped forward, but I grabbed his arm. "Let me handle this."

He pursed his lips, but nodded and stepped back. I took the forefront of this rescue mission and walked to the edge of the water. I leaned over the edge and cupped my hands together. "Hello!"

My voice echoed over the clearing. The water gurgled in reply. I straightened and frowned. She wanted to do it the hard way.

I picked up a stone and tossed it in the air to catch it in my palm. "Here goes nothing. . ."

I threw the stone. It landed with a hard ker-plop in the middle of the pond. A grin slid onto my face as the water gurgled. The familiar column of water burst into the air and exploded outward to reveal the beautiful woman. Her brilliant blue eyes looked from me to Cayden. The dragon lord knelt on one knee and bowed his head.

"Dragon of the Golden Fields. It is a pleasure to meet you," she greeted me.

He didn't lift his head. "The pleasure is all mine, My Lady."

She returned her attention to me. "Why have you come without your lord?"

I stepped forward so I stood at the edge of the pond. "Some red dragons attacked us at the Portal, and he got nicked by some poison on their claws. We need your water so we can heal him."

She tilted her head to one side and studied me. "Why do you seek the water?"

I frowned. "I already told you, it's because Xander's hurt. He's dying of poison right now, but the doc said you could cure him."

She walked across the water toward me. Every footstep left a small ripple in the still pond until she reached the rocks that ringed the pool. Her eyes caught mine as they had before. I couldn't move as she stepped off the last rock and stood within a foot of me.

Her eyes searched mine. "Why do you seek to save him?"

I swallowed the lump in my throat. It wasn't easy being this close to such an ethereal being. "Because he was hurt trying to protect me. I owe him one."

She cupped my cheek in one of her palms. Her skin was cold and brushed against mine like the flow of the gentle creek. "Is that all?"

It was hard to breathe so close to her overpowering aura. "Isn't that enough?"

She shook her head. "The power of my tears rests on the love of the one who seeks it. Without love there can be no cure." A small, sly smile slipped onto her lips a she tilted her head to one side. "Do you not love him?"

I pursed my lips and shook my head. "I don't know."

Her smile widened. She clasped her hands around mine and cupped my hands together. Her brilliant blue light pulsed from her hands. I felt a warmth enter my palms along with a weight. She released me and stepped back onto the rocks. I opened my hands and beheld a small vial of crystal-clear water.

I looked up at her and shook my head. "I don't understand. Why?"

She stepped backward into the pool. The water beneath her bubbled up and surrounded her, but her soft words reached me as clear as the water in my hands.

"Where there is doubt, there is still hope. Heal him and you will find the peace you seek."

My eyes widened. The water twisted upward and enveloped her. I stretched out my hand toward the woman. "Wait!"

The water swallowed her and retreated back into the pool. The woman was gone. I dropped my arm to my side and looked at the vial in my palm. The clear water sparkled in the dim light of early morning.

I clasped it tightly in my hand and turned to Cayden. He stood and looked from me to the vial. I took a deep breath and pocketed the vial. "Let's go."

We returned to the castle and the room. The grave faces were paler, as was Xander. I pulled out the vial. The group parted for me as I walked up to the bed. Xander's breathing was quick and shallow. He clutched the covers so tightly his hands were as white as the sheets.

I popped the cork and glanced at Cayden and the doctor opposite me. "Could you hold him still and get his mouth open for me?"

Cayden took the arms, Apuleius the legs, and the doctor pried open Xander's clenched teeth. I took a deep breath and rammed the mouth of the vial between his lips. The cool liquid slid out of the glass and into his mouth. He arched his back and his body tensed. I threw myself over his chest as he began to shake and thrash.

The episode lasted for a long few seconds before a soft blue glow spread from his chest across the rest of his body. The light passed under us, and we could feel the soothing coolness. It relaxed my muscles and my fear.

Xander's body relaxed and he fell back against the bed. We released him and stepped back to watch the light fully envelope him. The blue pulsed with a soft cold, but with each pulse it sank deeper into him. Soon the light disappeared. We waited with baited breath.

Xander's eyes fluttered open. He blinked at all of our tense faces. His eyes settled on me and widened. "Miriam-" He tried to sit up, but winced.

I grabbed his shoulders. "Easy there. I bet even dragons need to rest a bit after being almost-fatally poisoned."

He grabbed my arm and searched my face. "Is it you or some apparition come to take me to the skies?"

I smiled. "I'd have to go with the first option."

Xander pulled me down and pressed our lips together. I heard a gasp from Stephanie and a chuckle from Apuleius. We parted so I could partake of some air and wipe the blush from my cheeks.

"You could have just said 'thank you,'" I teased him.

He smiled. "I thought words would be too weak."

"Not as weak as you, My Lord," the doctor spoke up. He pulled the sheets over Xander's bandaged chest and up to his chin. "The poison may be vanquished, but your wounds from its talons are not yet healed."

Xander fell back against his pillows and shook his head. "You needn't worry too much for me, Galen. I hardly feel any weakness."

"But it is still a weakness, nonetheless, and I demand you get some rest," the doctor insisted. He swept his eyes over the many occupants of the room. "If you would all leave Our Lord may find some."

Xander nodded at me. "Let her stay. I must speak with her."

Galen bowed his head. "If you wish, My Lord."

CHAPTER 15

The room was vacated. I caught a smiling glance from Stephanie. The girl was getting bolder by the hour. When the door closed behind the last person I turned to Xander.

He stared at me with equal curiosity. "Did I imagine your falling into the Portal?" he wondered.

I shook my head. "Nope. I went back to my own world, but this-" I tapped my shoulder where my shirt hid my mark, "-told me something was wrong, so I came back."

He clasped one of my hands in his and pursed his lips. "Then it appears you have somehow overcome a Maiden's greatest enticement to remain with her dragon lord. You have managed to survive the Portal after the Marking." His hand fell away from mine and turned his head away from me. "Under the circumstances, I cannot in good faith keep you with me. You may return to your home."

I smiled and shrugged. "Why would I want to do that? I am home."

He whipped his head up and studied my face with flitting eyes. "Do you speak in earnest, or do you humor me in my recuperation?"

"You think I'd lie to you after I just saved your scaly skin?" I teased.

A grin brightened his face. He leaned forward and captured my lips in a searing kiss that spoke his happiness louder than any words. We broke apart so I could get some air. At this rate he was going to suffocate me. Even he was a little short as he studied me with his teasing smile.

I looked around the room and shrugged. "I mean, this isn't exactly a nice apartment, but it'll work."

He chuckled. "If I might tell the truth, the High Castle is not my home."

I stopped my perusing and curtain measurements to frown at him. "This isn't your place?"

He shook his head. "No. It is only a gathering place for we dragon lords, a place of compromise that sits at the point where our five kingdoms come together."

My mind imagined a stone hovel in some distant land. I cringed. "So where is your kingdom?"

"A moment and I will show you." He leaned back and pulled on the cord. The door soon opened and Darda stood in the doorway. "The map of the lands, if you will." She bowed her head and retreated, shutting the door behind her. He turned to me. "There is an excellent library here managed by those in the adjacent village. Within its collection are maps of the known world, and then some."

Darda soon returned with a roll of paper. I sat on the edge of the bed with my legs dangling over as she handed the paper to Xander. He unfurled the paper across his lap. A large, browned map spread out before him. The rough leather was covered from corner-to-corner with seas, mountains, oceans, lakes, and so much more.

Xander tapped on the center of the map where was scrawled the name High Castle. "This is where we are, and this-" he drew his finger across the map in a southwesterly direction, "-is my kingdom."

His kingdom was a large plain that abutted a large bay. A large dot sat on the bay, and the name on the map read 'Alexandria.'

He studied my expression. "Do you still wish to see my home?"

I looked up at him and grinned. "Why not? But-" I slid off the bed, "-first you need to obey the doctor's orders and get some rest."

Xander grabbed my arm. "Stay with me. I fear your return is but a dream, and I would not awaken without you at my side."

"Only if you're going to rest," I warned him.

He chuckled. "As you wish, My Maiden."

We slept together in his bed, and when the bright morning came I blinked against the harsh light. I willed my eyes open and looked up at the head of the bed.

It was empty.

I sat up and whipped my head left and right. My eyes found the objective of my design, and desire. Xander stood beside his dresser only half dressed. His chest was still bandaged, but the color of his skin was once more pinkish than white. He slipped his shirt on and turned to me with a teasing smile.

"Are you prepared for the journey?" he asked me.

I blinked at him. "For what?"

Xander chuckled and walked over to the bedside. He picked up the rolled-up map. "We have a great distance to travel before we reach my domain."

I frowned. "Is it that far to fly there?"

He shook his head. "No, but as I told you before the dragon form is a great strain on the body. That is why we will travel by horseback."

I winced and rubbed my behind. "Oh goody."

Xander tossed the map onto the unmade bed and wrapped his arms around my waist. He pressed me against him and looked into my eyes. "Do you doubt your decision to join me?"

I toyed with the strings that closed his shirt and smiled. "No, but I hope you enjoyed my butt. It might not make the trip."

Xander chuckled. "I will be sure to protect it as much as I can." There came a knock on the door. "Enter," he called out.

The door opened. Darda stood in the doorway and bowed to us. "My Lord, the horses are ready and Lord Cayden awaits you."

"Then that is our cue to leave," Xander announced. He looked to me. "I hope you won't be displeased with their following us. Cayden's kingdom abuts my own."

I shook my head. "Nope."

He grasped my hand and guided me to the door. "Then let us be off."

The hallways of the High Castle were alive with servants. They flitted to-and-fro, some with luggage in their arms and others returning for more. The servants stepped aside and bowed to us as we passed. Many of them snatched looks at us, and some of them weren't too friendly.

I stayed close to Xander's side and we navigated down to the courtyard. Horses and grooms filled the area, and somehow two dozen wagons fit into the space. People shouted and pointed, and others stumbled or rushed through the crowds. The luggage carriers dropped their loads into the wagons while the lords mounted on the horses watched over the proceedings.

In the chaos I saw the three other woman chosen as Maidens. Alex sat on a horse with the brown-bearded lord close beside her on his own sturdy steed. Close behind them on horses sat Olivia and Cindy, the first beside the dark-haired lord and the second close to the white-haired lord. Olivia looked as cross as ever, and I didn't catch any affection from her as she snatched glances at her lord.

Alex noticed me and waved her hand. "Miriam!" She urged her horse forward to us where she leaned down close to me and winked. "What do you think of my lord?"

I glanced past her at the bearded fellow. He sat proud and erect, and then belched. I winced. "He's-um, nice."

She grinned and winked at me. "Yeah, and nice in bed, too. And he's already promised to teach me how to ride all his stallions when we get to his castle." Her eyes flitted to Xander. "Not a bad catch yourself."

I smiled. "He'll do."

"Alex!" her lord bellowed.

Alex straightened and tightened her grip on the reins. "I'll make sure to write to you, and you do the same for me, okay? We might be stuck here, but we can at least enjoy it."

I nodded. "Sure thing, and have fun."

She laughed and turned her horse away. "Definitely!" She galloped away.

I furrowed my brow and looked to Xander. "Couldn't she go through the Portal like me?"

Xander pursed his lips. "You are the first of anyone from this world to survive the Portal's touch. I would not wish to see anyone else attempt the feat."

I arched an eyebrow. "So how did I live through it?"

He turned to me and gave me a teasing smile. "Because you are my Maiden."

I rolled my eyes and they found our two familiar companions. Stephanie and Cayden sat on a pair of fine tan steeds not too far from the gate. Beside them were two riderless white horses.

Xander offered me his arm. "Shall we?"

I grinned and accepted his offer. "Definitely."

And so began my adventures in this new world with my new dragon boyfriend.

A note from Mac

Thank you for purchasing my book! Your support means a lot to me, and I'm grateful to have the opportunity to entertain you with my stories.

If you'd like to continue reading the series, or wonder what else I might have up my writer's sleeve, feel free to check out my website at *macflynn.com*, or contact me at mac@macflynn.com.

* * *

Want to get an email when the next book is released? Sign up for the Wolf Den, the online newsletter with a bite, at *eepurl.com/tm-vn*!

Continue the adventure

Now that you've finished the book, feel free to check out my website at **macflynn.com** for the rest of the exciting series.

Here's also a little sneak-peek at the next book:

Realms of the Dragons:

> The life of a Maiden to a dragon didn't seem so glamorous. Actually, at that moment it was downright miserable.
> "A warm fire. An electric blanket. A roof over my head."
> That was my dream mantra as our group of two dozen riders rode through a torrential rain. All around us was a world of mud and thick forest. We were three days out from the High Castle, and ahead of us was another four days of outdoor fun. The dirt road we traveled on was now a mud pit fit for any hog. My cloak was soaked through and there were two puddles always with me, one in each of my riding boots.
> I could barely see ten feet in front of my horse's nose, and what I saw I didn't like. More rain. "A warm fire. An electric-"
> "Do you know how to create electricity?" Xander, my personal dragon lord, asked me. He rode close beside me, and in front of us were half our guards. Behind

us were the other half along with a few servants and our two friends, Stephanie and Cayden.

I raised my hooded head and arched an eyebrow at my dragon lord. "Do you even know what electricity is?"

He smiled and gave a nod. "Yes. Darda spoke often of your world when she first came into my mother's service. Her tales of electricity, power without physical force, have stayed with me."

"She's from my world?" I asked him.

He nodded. "Yes. The Portal is always open, and because of that people have been known to fall through. The rules demanded she not return to warn others, and so she was pressed into the service of the priests of the Portal until she was given to my mother."

I glanced over my shoulder at the short woman who followed behind us. Her stooped servile posture and primitive attire didn't bespeak of a person from my world. Still, that did explain her talk to we girls in the stable and about what we were leaving behind.

"So how long ago did she stumble into this place?" I asked him.

"Nearly sixty years ago."

I winced. That was a long time without electricity.

Xander stared ahead and pursed his lips. "I have long wished to see this magic of your world, and that is why I asked if you have knowledge enough to create this electricity."

I shook my head. "Nope, not a thing. I doubt I could create an electric shock by dragging my feet, much less enough that could power a light bulb or something simple like that."

Xander looked ahead of us and a small smile played across his lips. "Then I still must continue my dream."

I felt a little guilty at having dashed his hopes. "Maybe you can go there some day," I suggested.

He shook his head. "That is not possible. You yourself witnessed what would happen were I to even touch the Portal's surface."

"But I got through," I reminded him.

Xander returned his gaze to me and studied me. "Yes, but you are the first. I should not consider myself an exception to a rule that has stood a thousand years."

I wrinkled my nose. "So how come I'm an exception?"

He shook his head. "That is a mystery the priests could not solve and our books could not answer for us. However-" A teasing smile played across his lips, "-I would not have you make the attempt again."

I raised my head and saluted him. The raindrops nearly drowned me. "I promise I'll be a good little Maiden."

He chuckled. "I expect you to be something other than that, but I would ask nothing else of you."

I smiled, but the smile soon faded. Thinking about what I left behind reminded me of the rain. I huddled inside my wet cloak and shivered as the damp sank into my bones. The forest around us seemed so vast, and I felt like just a tiny, wet little speck in it.

Xander pulled his horse closer to mine and reached behind himself for his travel blanket. He let go of his reigns to drape the blanket across my shivering shoulders. The weight of the thick woolen blanket was preceded by the heat it trapped inside me.

I grabbed the front-top edges to keep the blanket on my slick shoulders and smiled at him. "Thanks." I glanced around us at the tall forest with its thick-trunked trees and undergrowth. "It feels like we've been in this place forever. How much farther do we have to go before we get out of this place?"

"The Viridi Silva is one of the largest forests in our world. We won't reach its southern boundary for another two days," he told me.

Xander looked at the guards ahead of us. Their heads were topped with rounded metal helmets and their hands were hidden by thick leather gloves with holes at the ends. They wore silver armor covered in cloaks, but I could see the armor had slits in the back near their shoulder blades. The look was similar to what the priest of the Portal had, and I knew what that meant.

"Are there any humans in this world besides the ones from mine?" I asked him.

Xander nodded. "Yes, but their settlements are few and far between. Many mated with dragons long ago and the dragon blood overrode their human line. Others have simply faded into history."

I glanced over my shoulder at Darda and Stephanie. "So we're kind of an endangered species here."

"I am afraid that is very close to the truth," he agreed. He straightened in his saddle and cleared his throat. "Spiros!"

The helmet of one of the guards was more elaborate than the others. Rather than a smooth top, his had a crest like the spine on a dragon's tail. He pulled his reigns back and turned toward us. The man was about thirty with a scar across his left cheek. His face was marred with care, but the corners of his lips had a hint of a smile. There was also a twinkle in his eyes that reminded me of Xander.

"You called, My Lord?" he shouted back.

Xander nodded. "Yes. I wish for your presence at my side for a moment." Spiros gave a few brief instructions to a young man of twenty who traveled at his side before he galloped over and joined us. Xander gestured to me. "I haven't properly introduced you to my Maiden. Miriam, this is my captain, Spiros."

His barely-concealed smile appeared as he bowed his head to me. "It is an honor to meet you, My Lady."

I nodded. "Ditto."

"Spiros and I grew up together, so do not be alarmed if he appears too impertinent," Xander warned me.

"If I am impertinent it is because I feel my advice will do you some good, My Lord," Spiros countered.

Xander chuckled. "Do me good? As when you coaxed me into riding my father's finest bull to see if its name of 'Devil' befitted it?"

"You rode him very well, My Lord, and no one doubted your bravery afterward," his captain argued.

"But some doubted very much I would survive my injuries," Xander pointed out.

I raised an eyebrow, all my discomfort forgotten. "Did the bull gore you?"

Spiro leaned forward so I could see him as he shook his head. "No, My Lady. The old king, My Lord's father, beat him quite profusely."

Xander winced at the memory and rubbed his arm. "I am ashamed to say I deserved as much. In riding the bull I had broken his strict order to stay away from the beast."

"So you see, My Lady, My Lord is in great need of my counsel to save him from his rash decisions," Spiros commented.

I snorted. "With friends like you who needs enemies?"

Spiros chuckled. "A very interesting saying, My Lady. I shall have to remember it."

"And wear it as a badge of honor, no doubt," Xander teased him. He leaned toward his friend and studied him with a sharp eye. "Though on the subject of good advice, I do recall your attempt to fly over the Grand Canal before your wings were softened."

"Softened?" I asked him.

"The wings of a dragon child are at first very hard and brittle," he explained to me. "The exposure of the wings to air and exercise softens the muscles and allows them to spread to their full length."

"If you will recall, My Lord, my father would not allow me to enter knight training until my wings were softened," Spiros spoke up. "I sought to show him that they had softened, at least far enough to support me."

Xander chuckled. "They had softened enough for you to fall into the Canal and nearly drowned yourself. If my guard escort had not found to where we had eluded them we would not be having this discussion."

I looked from Xander to Spiros. "You guys got away from the guards?"

Spiros's mischievous eyes flickered to his lord. "My Lord was very adept at eluding his keepers."

Any more conversation was cut off by a sudden worsening of the already-worse weather. The torrential rains fell faster and drowned out more than just the primitive road. I could barely hear myself think much less overhear the conversation between the two old friends. What I did catch, however, was a change in their expressions. They gazed out on the rains with pursed lips and furrowed brows before they glanced at each other with knowing looks. Spiros bowed his head and trotted off to retake his position at the head of the guards.

Cayden filled the empty spot vacated by Spiros, and Stephanie came up on his left side. "What do you make of this weather?" he shouted above the pounding rains.

Xander shook his head. "We cannot journey much farther than the bridge."

"If the bridge is to be had," Cayden pointed out.

There was no use talking at the top of our lungs, so the next couple of minutes was devoid of all but the thunderous rains that fell around us. The muddy road opened up ahead of us and revealed a small river. At least, small when there wasn't a flood warning. As we approached the waters I could hear the roar of the stream as it turned over the rocks in its bed and swept away the trees that lined its banks.

The bridge was a wooden makeup of logs strapped together with heavy rope and sealed with a tar-looking substance. Thick trees as wide as I was tall were the support beams that forced the bridge to curve over the water in a gentle arch. Below the arch were the fast waters of the wild river. I winced every time I heard a tree or rock slam into one of those pillars.

Spiros stopped his guards at the edge of the bridge. Xander trotted forward to stand beside his old friend and I cautiously followed. "I do not like this, My Lord," the captain shouted above the pounding rain.

Xander pursed his lips as he studied the bridge. The thick logs swayed side to side at each knock of their pillars. "We have little choice. There is no other bridge."

"Then allow my men and I to cross and test the logs, My Lord," Spiros pleaded.

Xander shook his head. "There is no time. The bridge may collapse at any moment. We cross now." He turned his horse so he rode perpendicular to the line and stood on his stirrups so all could see him. "We cross at once! Make two lines at two abreast and follow the rider in front of you!"

The riders grouped themselves into the long lines. I clutched my reigns and tensed my legs against the body of the horse. My steed threw its head back and whinnied.

Xander sidled up to my horse and leaned close to me. "Would you rather ride with me?"

I managed a shaky smile. "And miss all this fun? Not on your life."

He glanced past me at the roaring water beneath the bridge and frowned. I hardly heard his murmured words. "I pray not."

That's when an ear-splitting roar bashed my ears. I whipped my head to the left and upstream of the bridge. A huge tree with a six-foot trunk floated on the currents of the white-water waves.

"Across!" Xander yelled.

Too late. The tree bore down on the bridge, and us. It slammed into the left side and sank deep into the thick timbers. Many of the horses whinnied and reared up. My horse wasn't an exception. It reared up on both its back legs. One of the two remaining hooves slipped on the thick logs. The horse staggered backward and into the downstream wall. We hit it hard. I couldn't keep my position on the slick saddle and fell into the roaring abyss of the wild river.

Other series by Mac Flynn

Contemporary Romance
Being Me
Billionaire Seeking Bride
The Family Business
Loving Places
PALE Series
Trapped In Temptation

Demon Romance
Ensnare: The Librarian's Lover
Ensnare: The Passenger's Pleasure
Incubus Among Us
Lovers of Legend
Office Duties
Sensual Sweets
Unnatural Lover

Dragon Romance
Maiden to the Dragon

Ghost Romance
Phantom Touch

Vampire Romance
Blood Thief
Blood Treasure
Vampire Dead-tective
Vampire Soul

Werewolf Romance
Alpha Blood
Alpha Mated
Beast Billionaire
By My Light
Desired By the Wolf
Falling For A Wolf
Garden of the Wolf
Highland Moon
In the Loup
Luna Proxy
Marked By the Wolf
Moon Chosen
Continued on next page
Moon Lovers
Oracle of Spirits
Scent of Scotland: Lord of Moray
Shadow of the Moon
Sweet & Sour
Wolf Lake

Manufactured by Amazon.ca
Bolton, ON